BURIED IN PARADISE

A DESTINATION DEATH MYSTERY

CHARLEY MARSH

TIMBERDOODLE PRESS LLC

Buried in Paradise

Buried in Paradise is a work of fiction. The characters, incidents, and places are the product of the author's imagination or are used fictitiously. Any resemblance to actual events, locales, or persons living or dead is entirely coincidental.

Published 2021 by Timberdoodle Press LLC.

317 South 4th Street #366

La Crosse, WI 54601

Print Book ISBN# 9978-1-945856-72-3

Large Print ISBN# 978-1-945856-84-6

Cover Art: volare2004/depositphotos.com and Iurii/depostphotos.com

CHAPTER ONE

"Mizz Mun-row, look at me!"

Harriet Monroe, public relations director for the Island Resort, smiled and waved enthusiastically at the young girl as she rode by on her gaily painted lion. Hayley was part of the second group of orphans Harriet had brought to the island from stateside.

Generous corporate sponsors and private donations were making her pet project of giving orphans a break from the often crowded and bleak conditions of the country's orphanages a rousing success. They had already collected enough monies to fund the project through the end of the year. Even better, the orphan's scholarship fund was keeping pace, guaranteeing a solid education for every child who desired one in the field of their choice.

Harriet took a deep breath filled with the spicy perfume of exotic flowers and let it out on a contented sigh. Ocean breezes kept the beautiful island at a comfortable eighty degrees. The Island Resort was a true paradise and she was grateful to be working there, despite some recent difficulties.

"Whee!" Happy laughter filled the air. Along with her best friend, Solomon Hayes, and two other resort employees, Harriet had taken time from her other duties to escort ten of the group's twenty orphans to the resort's amusement park. She was minding three of the little girls who were riding the park's famous merry-go-round for the third time that morning.

The orphans were spending an entire week on the tropical island that was owned by the wealthiest man on the planet–her employer, the mysterious Douglas Wade. A man Harriet owed much to, but had yet to meet.

The resort hadn't been open long but was already booked solid for the next two years. Despite that, Wade had managed to make room for Harriet's orphans. She didn't know the particulars of how he had managed the feat–nor did she want to–because she'd probably feel guilty.

She imagined a few people had been told that

their reservations had been cancelled due to overbooking, or some other plausible excuse. However Wade had managed it, Harriet added the orphans to the growing list of things she kept in her head that she owed her employer for.

"Mizz Mun-row!" Hayley came around again, waving madly and bouncing on her lion's back.

Harriet smiled again and waved back. She never tired of seeing the happy expressions of her orphans. This particular little girl was a real cutie with expressive brown eyes, buttery smooth caramel skin, and a gap-toothed smile that seemed undimmed by her lot in life.

One of the hotel staff had taken time from her own busy day to plait Hayley's stiff black hair into dozens of braids that stuck out all over her head like sea urchin spines tipped with bright pink ribbons. From the way Hayley kept touching her head Harriet knew no one at the orphanage had taken the time to help the little girl with her hair.

"They look like they're enjoying my merry-go-round."

Harriet turned to look up at the man standing at her side. Even though she stood nearly six foot in bare feet, Harriet had to tilt her head back to see into Braxton Holliday's smiling green eyes.

"They love it, Brax. How could they not? You did an exquisite job restoring and painting the animals. Every child we've brought here through the orphan program gravitates to the merry-go-round for a ride, and most of them ride it every day."

Braxton's fleshy lips stretched into a pleased smile. At seven foot and three hundred fifty pounds, with a gleaming shaved head and large, meaty hands, the amusement park manager looked more bear than human, but Harriet knew he had a core soft as pudding.

The merry-go-round was Braxton's pride and joy. Over three hundred years old, it had taken him years to locate and restore the animals and other parts, and it was now the only merry-go-round in operation anywhere in the world. Harriet had recently featured it in a video ad for the resort, one of her favorite ads so far.

High-pitched screams pierced the air as a short train of roller coaster cars clanked and hummed over Harriet's head. Designed by Aldous, a friend of Douglas Wade's and the world's foremost authority on historic amusement parks, the roller coaster track towered over the entire park, climbing and winding and dropping through the other rides and amusements. The coaster's high points stood so far above Harriet's head that it hurt her neck to look up at them.

With its steep climbs and stomach rolling

drops it was easy to see why the coaster was a favorite with older children and adults alike.

Harriet refused to step foot on it.

Years before, when she and Solomon had been teenagers living on the streets of Portland, Maine, they had hitchhiked to a nearby beach town to eat salty potato fries and watch the amusement park rides. They had been dirt poor runaways at the time and couldn't afford to go on any of the rides–filling their bellies being much more important at the time–but Harriet never forgot the excitement and sounds of that park.

She could only imagine how exciting Braxton Holliday's park must look to the resort's visitors. The colorful park had something for everyone no matter what age. In addition to bumper cars, the park had a speedway track that circled the park's perimeter. The cars had magnetic fields that automatically fluctuated to prevent crashes, either into the low walls surrounding the track or another car.

There were gentle rides for the very young, and wild, whirly rides for older children and thrill seeking adults. Rides that whipped a person in dizzying circles and even one that dropped the brave from a hundred foot tower, only to be snapped back in a series of jerks from a thick bungee cord attached to their feet.

A soft breeze carried the scent of potato fries and grilled seafood from the food court on the edge of the park to Harriet. A resort guest could spend the entire day at the amusement park riding and eating, or they could simply relax on one of the many benches scattered through the park and watch others at play.

The merry-go-round's cheerful music wound down as it slowed to a halt. Hayley and her two companions climbed off their mounts and ran to Harriet.

"Did you see me, Miss Mun-row?" Haley asked, tugging on Harriet's hand.

Harriet placed her hand on the child's thin shoulder and gently squeezed. "I sure did. You looked magnificent riding that lion. Like the Queen of the Desert. What would you girls like to do next?"

The number of guests allowed at the resort at any one time were limited. That prevented crowding at any of the resort's attractions. No matter what the girls decided to do, there would be no waiting in long lines.

"I want to go down the water slide." Dorian, pale and freckled with violent red hair piped up in a thin, reedy voice.

"Yeah, water slide!" Hayley and Amber Lee,

the third of the trio of friends, grabbed Harriet's hands and pulled.

"How about we grab a lemonade on our way there?" Harriet said hopefully. She was thirsty but took her duties as child-minder seriously and hadn't wanted to leave the girls unattended to get something to drink.

"I luuuuv lemonade," Hayley assured her.

Five minutes later Harriet and her three charges made their way over the path of crushed white shells that wound through the rides, happily sipping on ice cold, tart-sweet lemonades. She listened to the young girls chatter about the merry-go-round animals as if they were live beasts and smiled to herself. Ah, to be that young and imaginative.

The roller coaster train made a brief appearance, darting out of a thick, green grove of something Harriet couldn't identify and disappeared again. She thought she spotted Solomon's pale blue shirt in the middle car. He had volunteered to take three of the older children on the roller coaster when they begged Harriet to go with them.

She would owe him for that. And knowing her friend, he would be sure to collect. Solomon never let her get away with anything.

A frown crossed her face as she thought about

her friend. She hoped he wasn't overdoing it. It wasn't that long ago since Solly had almost died when he'd stepped between her and the stream from a stun gun wielded by a desperate guest.

Most of the damaged nerves and muscle tissue in Solly's back left shoulder had been replaced. Fortunately the stream from the gun had missed any vital organs. Physical therapy had worked its magic as well, but her friend still wasn't back to one hundred percent.

Solly never complained, but Harriet knew her closest friend inside and out. She could tell he still felt the effects of the injury. He also still had scar tissue, but he had decided to wait on plastic surgery, joking that the scars made him look like a badass.

And wouldn't he read her the riot act if he knew she still worried about him?

Harriet forced her thoughts back to the present. Small flowering shrubs covered in brilliant red and orange blossoms and rough-barked palm trees edged the wide path, screening it from the various rides.

Tiny, colorful birds flitted through the greenery. Brilliant green geckos darted around the palm trunks looking for prey, bobbing up and down, their bright eyes missing very little. Iridescent green and blue insects gathered pollen from large showy hibiscus blossoms.

Her little group came to a fork in the path. One fork led to the water slide, the other circled back through the park to the entrance. Wooden signs identified the paths.

"Can anyone tell me what the signs say?" Harriet asked. She dropped her empty lemonade cup into one of the park's many discreetly placed trash receptacles.

"It says . . ." Dorian scrunched her face and pointed. "That one says wa-ter-sl-ide. Water slide! That way to the water slide! Come on!" She grabbed Hayley and Amber Lee's hands and all three girls took off down the path, their thin legs flashing in the sun.

Harriet picked up the girls' dropped cups and added them to the trash bin. She knew she should scold them but decided now was not the time. She would bring up the subject of littering later and gently remind them that they needed to pick up after themselves.

She had discovered with her first group of orphans that it was difficult for them to grasp the degree of freedom they had on the island. They were used to a strictly regimented, austere life with more scolding than encouragement and few joys. As far as Harriet was concerned this week was all about bringing more joy into their difficult lives.

She set off down the water slide trail after the girls at a fast walk. Each attraction or ride at the amusement park had two employees monitoring it so Harriet wasn't worried about their safety. Other than the occasional murder, the resort had yet to lose a guest.

Most of the resort's employees had volunteered to watch over the orphans so the children wouldn't have to stay together. The extra volunteers meant a child could do whatever they wanted during their week's stay. The island had much to offer in addition to the amusement park.

The marina with every water sport toy known to man and the Angel Brothers Circus were popular destinations, as was the pristine beach that ran along the southern half of the western side of the island. Most of the orphans came from inner city neighborhoods and had never seen an ocean, let alone a beach of fine white sand. They were understandably giddy with the discovery that there was more to the world than what little they had experienced in their short lives.

Rounding a corner of lush vegetation, Harriet suddenly popped out of the jungle into a sunny clearing. The large water slide, with its labyrinth of twisting, open and covered camouflaged tubes, was part of a natural waterfall. The waterfall fed into a clear lagoon that had been altered only slightly to create shallower landing spots for the slides.

Water droplets from the waterfall's spray shimmered and sparkled in the sunlight, fracturing into miniature rainbows that formed and disappeared and formed again. Tiny lizards and birds, vibrant with color, darted through the lagoon's surrounding jungle.

The water slide was the one place in the park where the roller coaster didn't invade. The lush growth surrounding the lagoon drowned out the noise from the rest of the park and created a peaceful oasis set with well spaced benches for sitting.

Harriet waved to the water slide attendant sitting at the base of the waterfall, his feet dangling in the lagoon. The girls were already scrambling up the subtly stepped rocks to the left of the natural waterfall. Another attendant waited for them at the top to help them into the slide.

Harriet chose a bench where she could help keep an eye on the girls and made herself comfortable. The waterfall made a dull roar as it hit the lagoon, sending up a spray of fine mist. Birds sang and insects buzzed. The gentle tropical breeze rattled palm fronds over Harriet's head. The combination of mountain water and lush jungle kept the sunny spot comfortably cool.

"Mizz Mun-row! Watch me!" Hayley shouted down from the top of the waterfall. Dorian and Amber Lee waved from the openings of the two remaining slides. It looked as if the girls were going to race to the bottom.

Harriet knew that even though the three chutes criss-crossed each other several times, they were well separated at the bottom so all three girls could shoot out at the same time without fear of landing on top of each other.

"I'm watching!" Harriet shouted back. She gave a double thumbs up sign and settle back to wait for the girls to reappear at the bottom.

Amber Lee and Dorian popped up in the lagoon several minutes later but there was no sign of Hayley. Harriet jumped to her feet. The lagoon attendant was on his feet, wading towards the spot where Hayley should have appeared.

"Do you see her?" Harriet called. Fear clutched at her heart. She knew the water in the slide was shallow, making drowning difficult. But what if Hayley had bumped her head somehow?

"No." The attenant shook his head. "She should have popped out by now, unless she deliberately stopped herself. The kids do that sometimes. The slide is clear until it reaches the last ten feet, so you feel like you're inside the waterfall. It's pretty cool. You should try it." The attendant didn't sound worried at all.

Harriet relaxed slightly. There wasn't anything in the slide to hurt Hayley. The attendant most likely had the right of it, Hayley had spread her hands and feet to stop her slide down the tube.

"I wonder how long she can hold herself up there?"

The attendant shrugged. "She's young so probably not more than a few minutes. There's a sharp curve on a fairly level section of the tube that's a little slower. My guess is that's where she is. I'll go–" he stopped talking abruptly.

"What is it?" And then Harriet saw for herself. An adult-sized body had popped out of the end of the slide, followed immediately by a scowling Hayley.

"That man blocked my slide," she complained as she waded toward the edge of the lagoon. "I had to push him to make him get going. I want to go again."

Harriet barely heard her. She was staring in horror at the body floating face down in the lagoon. A body with a massive dent in the back of its head.

CHAPTER TWO

Harriet suppressed a shudder at the thought of Hayley stuck inside the water slide with a dead man. Thank heavens the little girl hadn't realized the man blocking her progress was dead. Harriet frowned at the body floating face down near the end of the slide. She didn't want the girls to see the dead man but she knew better than to move the body.

"Call Alex Hayes," she told the attendant quietly. "And let Braxton know. Don't let anyone near the slide until Alex gets here. Tell him I've taken the girls to the circus." She didn't care for the excited gleam in the attendant's eyes.

"You did it again," he said, pointing at the body in the lagoon. "Maybe we should start calling you the Angel of Death." He lost the grin and cleared his throat when Harriet glared at him.

"Sorry," he mumbled. "I make bad jokes when I'm nervous and dead people make me nervous."

Harriet didn't bother to answer. If she was honest, she did feel like an angel of death in a way. This man made the fifth body in as many months–all found by her or someone she was with. It was uncanny and not a little frightening the way bodies seemed to turn up wherever she happened to be.

Shaking off the morbid bent of her thoughts, Harriet turned her attention back to the girls. She needed to get them away from the water slide before they realized the man was dead and freaked out. The week was supposed to be a fun break for them, not a reminder of how fragile life was. It definitely wasn't supposed to be a new source of nightmares.

"Girls! Wait!" Harriet waded out of the lagoon and hurried around to the bottom of the steps. What could she tell them? They would not be happy about having to leave the water slide.

"I'm sorry," she began. "There's a problem with the slide and they have to do some maintenance on it. Why don't we head over to Angel Brothers Circus while they do their work? It shouldn't take long. We'll come back here later today or tomorrow. Okay?"

The joy on the girls' faces shut down so quickly it made Harriet want to cry and rant at the same time. Life could be so unfair at times. She looked for a way to put the happy back in their day.

"I promise we'll come back. Okay?" She searched their faces. "I promise," she repeated. "As soon as they tell me the slide is fixed. And I never break a promise."

The girls grumbled a bit but turned around and descended the steps.

"Can we come back today?" Hayley asked.

"If they can fix the problem today then we will definitely come back today," Harriet assured her. "In fact I'll leave a message with Braxton Holliday to call me when the water slide is open again and I'll come find you."

"Even if we're in bed?" Amber Lee asked.

Of mixed heritage, Amber Lee was the smallest and most delicate looking of the three friends. Her almond shaped eyes held a look of skepticism far beyond her years. None of the orphans had what could be even remotely thought of as a good story. Amber Lee's was more tragic than most.

Her entire family, including an older brother and younger sister, had been slaughtered in a gang dispute. According to the report Harriet had read, Amber Lee had survived only because her mother had sent her to the store for something unimportant. Amber Lee had returned to an apartment filled with blood and bodies and called the police.

Despite how little time Harriet had spent in Amber Lee's company, she had come to respect the young girl's poise and intelligence.

Harriet crossed her heart with her finger. "Cross my heart and hope to die. As soon as I hear from Braxton I'll come find you. It won't be in the middle of the night though–the amusement park closes at eleven. Even the attendants have to eat and sleep."

"Then we'll have to ride the slide tomorrow." Hayley shrugged at her friends. "Come on. Let's go see the circus!"

The girls joined hands again and headed back down the path at a run.

"Wait for me, girls!" Harriet jogged after them. A young, female park employee was putting up a "Closed For Maintenance" sign over the water slide sign when they reached the fork in the path. The girls stopped.

"You'll have to make that man leave too," Hayley told the employee. "He was still in the lagoon. We're going to the circus now but we'll come back when the slide is fixed."

"They're going to have to pull that man out of the lagoon," Amber Lee told Hayley. "He was dead."

Harriet's eyes widened. "Why would you say that, Amber Lee?" She hadn't realized that the young girl had gotten a good look at the body. Surely she wasn't close enough to see the damage to the back of the man's skull.

"He *had* to be dead Miss Monroe," Amber Lee explained, her voice matter of fact. "He was either dead or he could hold his breath for a really, really long time."

"Huh." Like Harriet had thought, the girl was observant and intelligent. Not much escaped those watchful eyes.

The attendant smiled at the girls. "The circus is great. You'll have fun. Be sure to come back and use the water slide after we fix the problem."

"We will!" all three girls assured her.

Harriet directed them down the fork opposite the one they'd used to get to the slide so they wouldn't have to walk back through the center of the park. The path led them to the amusement park's outer boundary and then followed the inside edge of the race track around to the entrance gate.

They could hear the merry-go-round music and happy screams from the other rides. Harriet wondered where Solly was. She'd have to call him once she got the girls away from the park.

The resort's security director, Alex Hayes, and his assistant Tarbell Fox arrived at the gate just as Harriet was passing through with the girls.

"Girls, why don't you go pick out a cart and wait for me? I need to speak to Mr. Hayes and Mr. Fox a minute."

A dozen hydrogen powered chrome and resort blue carts sat in the amusement park lot, available for any guest to take and use. The carts ran silently, had a top speed of thirty miles an hour, and were located all over the western side of the island.

"What happened, Harry?" Tarbell Fox, an ex-Boston detective, smiled when the girls began to argue over which one of the identical carts was the best. He lost the smile and touched Harriet lightly on the arm. "Quite the kerfuffle, I understand. Are you okay?"

Harriet shook her head. She liked Tarbell a lot. The burly, red-haired Irishman was a good friend and fun to be with. His penchant for speaking in old-fashioned jazz slang entertained her even though it often confused her.

Alex had yet to speak, but she knew he was watching her–she could feel the weight of his gaze pressing against her. She avoided looking at him, focusing her attention on Tarbell instead, but she was acutely aware of the man she loved. And of the anger she still felt toward him.

There were unresolved issues between her and Alex–well, only one. One *really* big unresolved issue. Alex, she knew, wanted to talk it through, but Harriet had been thrown off balance and until she regained her equilibrium she *couldn't* talk about it.

How was she supposed to react to learning that her mind had been purposefully wiped of every memory concerning the first eight years of her life?

She realized Tarbell was still waiting for an answer. She shook her head again.

"Not really, no. I'm not okay. We were having a great time at the merry-go-round. Then the girls decided they wanted to try the water slide. All three climbed to the top and took the slide down, only Hayley got hung up inside the right hand tube where it turns a sharpish corner. I was just about to go after her when a man's body popped out with Hayley right behind it."

"Briny." Tarbell gently squeezed Harriet's arm in sympathy and let it go. "If you need to blow your top later give me a call. We can hit the fillmill."

Harriet translated. Briny meant unpleasant. Blow your top was to let off steam. "Fillmill?" she asked.

"The bar, Harry. I'll stand you a drink at the bar in the hotel."

"Oh. Fillmill. Got it. Thanks, Tar, but I'll be okay."

"We'll need you to drop by the security office and give a formal statement." Alex's tone was brisk and businesslike. He felt that he'd been patient long enough, waiting for Harriet to look at him.

He didn't like being ignored. He especially didn't like being ignored by Harriet.

"Bring Hayley. We'll need a statement from her as well." Alex knew that Fox wasn't hitting on his girl, but he still felt a surge of jealousy because she was talking to Fox and not to him and that made him sound surly.

Harriet let herself look at Alex then and wished she hadn't. His piercing eyes, the same color as the deep blue North Atlantic on a sunny day, were focused intently on her face. His ruggedly handsome face was so familiar to her.

The white scar over his right eyebrow. His crooked nose. Those talented, sensuous lips that sent shivers of pleasure down her spine.

Harriet's heart skipped a beat and she swallowed against the sudden lump in her throat. She had missed him terribly. They hadn't spoken in a week. She had refused to answer his calls and deleted his text and voice messages. She hadn't even seen Alex except from a distance–ever since Alex and her friend Payson Douglas had dropped their bombshell on her.

Since that day, that horrid afternoon in Payson's cottage, whenever she saw Alex coming Harriet turned and went the opposite way, coward that she was. She had even missed her weekly Thursday lunch date with Payson, something that she had always looked forward to with happy anticipation. Payson was like a much loved, favorite uncle to Harriet and she cherished their friendship. Now that friendship felt strained and she didn't know what to say to either man.

A sharp shooting pain shot through Harriet's skull. She saw Alex's gaze sharpen and knew he saw the pain. And he knew the reason for it.

She resisted rubbing her head. "I have to go," she muttered.

Harriet turned away from the two men and walked toward the girls as fast as she could without breaking into a run. Pasting a smile on her face, she got them settled into their chosen cart and headed for the circus.

Alex resisted the urge to go after her. Frustrated beyond measure, he watched the woman he loved drive away. He wanted to marry and raise a family with Harriet Monroe, but there were things from her past that needed to be dealt with first.

Painful, horrible things that Harriet needed to face if she was ever going to be free of the pain in her skull. Things that had been hidden from her since she was a young girl almost the same age as her little orphan girls.

He and Payson had taken the first step toward getting Harriet help by telling her that her memory had been intentionally wiped by the aunt who took Harriet in after her parents died. The conversation hadn't gone well. Since then Harriet had refused to see or speak to either him or Payson.

With a heavy inward sigh, Alex focused his thoughts on the problem at hand.

"Let's go get an identity on the body and see if we can keep this one out of the media news feed."

"Good luck with that." Fox followed Alex through the park gate. "I'm betting word has already leaked. Did you know the media has picked up the resort employees' nickname for the island? Everyone refers to us as Destination Death now."

Alex's eyes cut sideways toward Fox. "Well, it seems they aren't far wrong, are they?" he said grimly.

CHAPTER THREE

Within minutes of driving away from the amusement park–and Alex–the pain in Harriet's head vanished. She forced herself to focus on the girls. Her own problems could wait. Showing the orphans a good time was all that mattered. She tuned in to their high, thin, little girl voices and grinned. They were arguing over the merits of their chosen merry-go-round animal. The imaginations of the young never ceased to amaze her.

Harriet spotted the long resort-blue banner that topped the main circus tent flying above the treetops and pointed it out to the girls.

Angel Brothers had been late coming to the Island Resort because of previous commitments, but once set up the circus had quickly become a favorite entertainment, especially with the younger resort guests. The circus still toured the European continent for five months of the year during the warmer summer season, and many of the resort guests with children made a point to book their stay while the circus was on the island.

Unlike during the Angel Brothers European tour, the more intimate island setting gave the resort guests the opportunity to see acts being developed and a chance to interact with the performers.

Founded in the early 1600s by four acrobats known as the Angel Brothers even back then, the circus was the longest running family-owned business still operating anywhere in the world. It was also the only circus still in business. Only one of the original brother's descendants was still associated with the circus, but one family member was enough to keep the circus's streak alive.

That family member was Madame Zaza, the circus's fortune teller and tarot card reader. Dark eyed and raven haired, Madame Zaza ruled the circus with an iron fist–no velvet glove in sight. As the only remaining direct descendent, Zaza's word was law.

Harriet found the fortune teller mysterious and not a little intimidating.

No one admitted to knowing the fortune teller's age. Rumored to be anywhere between forty and eighty-five, it was impossible to tell her age by looking at Zaza. With her golden turban, flowing, colorful robes, and her slim arms decorated with dozens of gold and silver bangles, she looked the spitting image of how an old-fashioned fortune teller should look.

Harriet hoped she could avoid the fortune teller's tent. Her sole visit there several months before had been upsetting in ways that remained clouded in her memory. Madame Zaza had insisted on telling Harriet's fortune, a reading that left Harriet with more questions than it gave answers.

"Do they have animals here, Miss Monroe?"

Dorian's question snapped Harriet from her reverie. "Yes they do, Dorian." She smiled at the little redhead. "Would you like to see the animals?"

A chorus of excited yesses answered her. She imagined the girls had seen only dogs, pigeons, feral cats, and rats in the city. Even the horses the security police had ridden for two hundred years had been replaced with motorized bicycles.

"Hello, Tamara." Harriet greeted the circus gate keeper. Although access to everything on the island was included in the resort fee, the gate keepers were there to answer questions or provide help when needed.

The gatekeepers kept an eye on everything, anticipating problems before they got out of hand. Tamara had prevented three teenage boys from releasing the circus monkeys only the week before. "I saw the gleam in their eyes," she told Harriet later. "I knew they were up to something and had them followed."

Harriet parked the cart, warned the girls to stick with her, and sighed when they leaped out of the cart and ran for the gate. It was hard to fault such enthusiasm.

"Good morning, Harry. Who did you bring us for a visit today?" The circus's attractive young greeter smiled at Harriet and the girls. Tamara's sparkly, emerald green skinsuit hugged her curvy body and matched her large, expressive eyes.

"This is Hayley, Dorian, and Amber Lee." Harriet briefly touched the shoulder of each girl as she named her.

"We were on the water slide but we had to leave because there was a dead man in the lagoon." Amber Lee reached out to touch Tamara's skinsuit. "Pretty. When I grow up I want to wear one just like yours."

Tamara raised her eyebrows at Harriet. "A dead man?" she mouthed.

Harriet grimaced and shrugged one shoulder.

"He was blocking my slide." Hayley not-so-subtly nudged Amber Lee aside so she could get Tamara's full attention. "I had to push him out of the way. He made me lose the race. Do you have lions here?"

Tamara wiped the look of shock from her face and squatted down in front of Hayley. "We have two lions. They are very fierce but our lion tamer won't let them hurt you, I promise."

Harriet knew that the circus's lion tamer, Sugo, had raised and trained the circus's orphaned pair of lions from when they were small cubs. She had watched him interact with the lions when they weren't performing and understood that they were his family. With Sugo, when there was no one to impress, the lions acted more like docile house pets than the kings of the African plains.

"I tamed the lion on the merry-go-round," Hayley told Tamara solemnly. "He looks mean and scary but he isn't really. I bet your lions are just like that."

"You'll have to visit them and see for yourself. The next show starts in twenty minutes." Tamara stood and smiled at Harriet. "No more bodies today, all right?" she whispered. "Seems like everywhere you go they turn up."

Harriet rolled her eyes and led the girls through the gate.

Where the amusement park was all about colorful motion, the circus was colorful mystery, games, and traditional circus treats. The smell of buttery popcorn, hot dogs, and cotton candy greeted the group.

A stilt walker spotted the girls and approached them. Dressed in a bright red and white striped jacket and pants, he towered over the small knots of guests wandering the grounds. When he reached Harriet and her charges he leaned down, made a flower appear seemingly from thin air, and handed Dorian the bright red paper flower.

"A gift to match your fabulous hair," he said solemnly.

Dorian clutched the flower to her chest, her eyes shining with pleasure.

"I'm Harry Monroe, the resort's public relations director," Harriet said. "You wouldn't happen to have two more of those flowers for Dorian's friends, would you?"

She was always careful to make sure all of her orphans received equal treatment while on the island. While some children were simply easier to like and be around than others, Harriet felt it was important to show no preferential treatment. Life was difficult enough for the girls without stirring up jealousies and hard feelings.

"I sure do." The stilt walker produced two more blossoms with a flourish and handed one to Hayley and one to Amber Lee. "Three beautiful flowers for three beautiful girls."

The girls giggled and took the offered blossoms. The stilt walker waved his hand a fourth time and another blossom appeared. Handing it to Harriet with a deep bow, he introduced himself.

"I am Lino Angel, at your service. Now you will be as beautiful as your little angels."

Charmed by the gesture, Harriet smiled and thanked Lino. Taking the flower, she tucked it behind her ear and led the girls deeper into the circus.

A large red and white striped tent dominated the center of the circus grounds. The food and games were housed in square bamboo and thatch structures and small, bright blue and white striped cabanas that circled the main tent. Harriet led the girls to a cabana she knew sold ice cream and ordered them each a cone.

The girls licked happily at their cones as they made their way around the large central tent toward its entrance. By the time they'd reached it the cones had been devoured and the girls were ready to watch the show. They fairly quivered with excitement. Dressed in their bright new clothes, the girls reminded Harriet of gaily colored balloons boouncing on the end of a string.

Rather than the traditional three ring affair that the circuses of old held, the Angel Brothers held their show in one central ring. Short, tiered bleachers surrounding most of the ring ensured everyone got a seat with a good view of the activity in the center.

Because of the limited number of guests at the resort on any given day, the circus was never crowded. Harriet knew from talking with her friend Payson that the Angel Brothers had been busy working out several new tricks and acts. She wondered if they would see one today.

The resort manager had confided to Harriet that the guests loved the fact that they got an exclusive preview of the evolving acts because it gave them bragging rights back home.

The circus loved that they had a free winter home as well as early feedback on whether the concept and execution for new acts were working or not.

"Let's sit here!" Hayley led the way to a set of bleachers and plunked her small body down on the bottom level. The other two girls sat on either side of her and Harriet took a seat on the row behind them. The lights went off just as she settled, plunging the tent into absolute darkness until a single spotlight panned over the center ring.

A white horse carrying a petite woman entered the ring and cantered around the outer edge. The spotlight followed the pair around the ring, reflecting off the woman's glittering red skinsuit. She rode bareback, back straight, relaxed and graceful. The only sound in the tent was the steady cadence of thudding hooves in the soft sand that filled the ring.

Even the girls were quiet, mesmerized by the horse passing within a few feet of where they sat. Soon a man on a matching white horse joined the woman. The entire ring lit up. The show had begun.

The girls sat silent except for gasps of astonishment, too enthralled to speak. Every once in a while Harriet would catch a glimpse of the expressions of wonder on their wide-eyed faces as a variety of acts played out before them.

It was hard to think about dead bodies while watching the circus's expert entertainers. The circus was definitely providing the distraction Harriet needed for the girls.

The girls squealed with pleasure when Sugo and his two lions finally appeared. Harriet thought Hayley would burst from her skin with excitement when Sugo asked for a volunteer and invited Hayley into the ring to help him with a trick. Her warm brown eyes still sparkled with excitement when they emerged from the tent after the show.

Harriet smiled as she listened to Hayley tell her two friends about touching one of the lions–it's fur was soft as a kitty's and they smelled funny and their teeth were enormous! To hear Hayley, the girl was now an expert on lions.

One of the things that had surprised Harriet when she began bringing orphans to the island was how entertaining children could be. She had never spent much time around kids until her first group of orphans, and she hadn't anticipated how much fun she would have hanging out with them.

The girls constantly surprised her with their intelligence–had she been as smart when she was their age? Somehow she didn't think so. The joy the girls took from even the smallest, most insignificant thing was infectious.

"Are you hungry, girls? Should we get something to eat while we're here or would you rather wait until you get back to the hotel?"

"Here!" They chorused.

"I want popcorn!"

"I want cotton candy!"

"More ice cream!"

Harriet laughed. "Okay. How about if we get a veggie wrap first, then we can have all those things." She led the girls around the large tent toward the food tents in the rear.

Once they had food and drinks in hand she found a wide bench that would hold the four of them and settled everyone to enjoy their meal. The girls ate happily, talking and pointing out the games they'd like to try after they ate.

The sun felt warm on Harriet's face and shoulders. Despite the knowledge that the resort had another body to deal with, she felt a sense of contentment wash over her as she ate her wrap and listened to the girls chat.

Harriet had purposefully steered her trio to the far side of the central big top, out of sight of Madame Zaza's fortune reading tent, in the hope that she wouldn't have to see Madame Zaza again. She knew her discomfort was foolish, but every time she thought about Madame Zaza her hands grew clammy and her head started to hurt.

"I really have a phobia about that woman," she muttered, scrunching up the paper from her sandwich.

"What? What woman? What's a phobia?" Beside Harriet, Amber Lee looked puzzled.

"No one. Never mind. I was thinking about

something else, Amber Lee." Harriet suppressed a groan. She hadn't meant to speak out loud.

Amber Lee assumed a wise air. "Phobias are grown-up stuff, right?"

"Right." Harriet hesitated. She really should take advantage of the teaching moment. "Actually no. Anyone of any age can have a phobia. A phobia is when you are afraid of something. Really, *really* afraid. Like if a person totally freaks out whenever they see a spider. You could say that person has a spider phobia."

"I have a snake phobia." Dorian shuddered.

Harriet nodded. "Lots of people have phobias about snakes. I'm not very fond of them myself. People have phobias about flying, or being way up high. Anything frightening.

"Are you girls almost ready to try your luck at some games?"

Harriet gathered up everyone's trash and told the girls to wait on the bench for her while she located a recycle barrel. Arms loaded, she spied one between two nearby food cabanas. As she was depositing her load she heard someone talking behind one of the tents.

"Why did you have to . . ." The rest of the sentence was lost. ". . . I told you to leave Davis to me." Even though the speaker spoke in low tones he sounded furious. Harriet paused to listen.

"He wanted to cut me out. I know it. You should have heard the way he spoke to me." A second man sounded bitter and just as angry. "What happened wasn't my fault."

Harriet froze. Who was Davis and what had happened? She strained to hear more.

"Three bodies can cover a lot more ground than two can. It will take us twice as long without Davis's help. Not to mention that you failed to recover his half of the map. The *important* half, I might add."

"Yeah, well you weren't there. Don't forget I'm the one who tracked down the diary and the other half of the map. At least I got us here."

"Keep throwing that in my face and see what happens," hissed the first speaker. "Do you have any idea how much trouble you've made for us? You didn't even make sure Davis had the map on him–"

"Are you threatening–"

"Mizz Mun-row! We're ready to play games!" Three little girls appeared between the tents.

The voices fell silent. Harriet finished depositing their trash and hurried toward the girls. "All right then, what do you want to play first?"

As she herded the girls toward the game huts she kept her eyes peeled for two people walking out from between the tents but nobody appeared.

Harriet soon forgot about the conversation behind the tents. The girls were having a grand time trying to best each other at the ring toss and other games. She tried to keep the dismay she felt from her face when they decided shooting modified lasers at moving targets was the most exciting game on offer. She bit her tongue and reminded herself that these girls had all either grown up with or had been exposed to violence. For them it was simply another aspect of life.

Eventually all three girls had won prizes. The afternoon had flown by and they were obviously worn out and fighting it. Braxton had tagged Harriet to let her know the water slide was open again but she didn't tell the girls. It would be better to start fresh tomorrow after a good night's sleep.

She brought three sleepy eyed girls back to the hotel and turned them over to a hotel maid who had volunteered to take the girls to dinner and then spend the night with them.

Normally each group of four orphans shared a two bedroom, two bath suite with an adult providing overnight supervision, but the fourth member of Hayley's group had asked to sleep with another set of girls her age and an extra bed had been set up for her, leaving Hayley and her friends to happily sleep together in one king size bed.

Harriet had considered putting the group of twelve orphans up in two of the resort's stand alone cottages, but the cottages were too far from the main hotel and the orphans would need someone to cook for them as well as stay with them.

So far, putting them in the hotel had worked really well. It was convenient for the staff who volunteered to help out with the girls and the girls seemed to love their luxury suites.

At first Harriet had been worried about finding enough people to help with the orphans, but there had been no shortage of staff volunteers. Everyone who worked for the resort wanted to help out in any way they could.

The whole undertaking was working out far better than she could have imagined, with the added bonus of bringing different staffing groups together that normally didn't interact. Kitchen and restaurant staff were meeting and forging friendships with the hotel, marina, and maintenance crews. The resort was benefitting from the orphan program in ways Harriet had never imagined.

Soon it would be time to risk bringing a group

of orphan boys to the island now that they had a system in place to deal with the children.

It wasn't that Harriet didn't like little boys. She just knew, and her friend Solly had confirmed, that they would likely be more difficult.

Boys couldn't help how they behaved, Solly had explained to her, it was in their DNA. Boys needed to push boundaries–to test their limits–and in doing so, test themselves. That usually meant getting into some form of trouble.

All of the orphans, boys and girls, were damaged in some way simply because of the circumstances. Most had never known the support of two loving parents. Many had been abused. Most never had enough to eat before being absorbed into an orphanage. Life for them so far had been an ordeal to be endured and hopefully survive.

Harriet wanted to give these children hope. She wanted to show them that there was something to reach for beyond just surviving. She wanted to show them that there was a wide world filled with possibilities and good people. She wanted her orphans to understand that her program didn't stop after their week on the island.

They could go ahead and dream. They could explore those possibilities and opportunities. There would be mentors and counselors available whenever needed to help guide them.

Harriet wished someone had done something like that for her. Life would have been so much easier. She shook off the nagging thought that maybe someone *had* done something similar for her–that somewhere in those lost memories lay something very, very important.

CHAPTER FOUR

"Good afternoon, Harry. I didn't think you were coming in to the office today." The male droid manning the high wooden reception desk in Harriet's office lobby greeted her with a wide smile.

She ran her eye over the British droid's impeccable pale blue linen suit. A triangle of crisp white cotton peeked over the edge of his chest pocket.

She swore the dapper droid dressed better than most of the resort's wealthy guests. It had taken her a while to train him to call her Harry although he still insisted on calling her Miss Monroe when others were around.

Jeeves might be considered only a droid by most, but Harriet had discovered that he was a droid with a definite personality. A top of the line model easily mistaken for being human, Harriet treated him like she would anyone else.

"Hi, Jeeves. How was your day? I only stopped by for a few minutes. I wanted to check on any messages you might have for me and pick up my video camera. I'll be out of the office again tomorrow."

Jeeves' straight white teeth gleamed in another smile. "My day was fine. Thank you for asking. I have one message for you from Mr. Payson Douglas. He asks that you please call him at your earliest convenience. He misses you."

Harriet blushed. She had avoided Payson ever since the day he and Alex had confronted her and told her that her aunt and uncle had had her memory wiped of everything before her eighth year. As she had done with Alex's calls, she had deleted Payson's calls without answering. Cowardly, but there you have it.

"Anything else?"

"Yes. Mr. Hayes stopped by. He would like you to stop by the security office to give a statement, also at your earliest convenience."

The wonderful thing about droids was, they never showed curiosity or passed judgement. Under the circumstances Harriet felt grateful for that little fact. She thanked Jeeves and headed for the hallway that led to her office.

Jeeves hurried over and unlocked the secured hallway door for her with a flourish. His blue eyes seemed to twinkle in his vid-star handsome face. "Let me know if I can be of any further service, Harry."

Harriet slipped through the door and heard the lock click in place behind her. She heaved a sigh of relief. It was the first time she'd been alone since leaving her cottage that morning.

She stood for a moment without moving and let herself enjoy the quiet. Fans turned slowly overhead with a soft whir. The hall's creamy tile floor remained cool in the tropical heat. Tall and narrow, the tinted windows on the left looked out on the pale pink crushed shell road and the long, low kitchen building set behind the offices.

A vibrant fresco of the island painted by a renowned local artist dominated the hall's right hand wall. The door to Harriet's office was camouflaged in a bright blue ribbon of a waterfall. The waterfall reminded her of the water slide and the dead body.

She heaved a sigh as she placed her palm on the security reader and punched in her code. The door slid open, revealing a light, airy office decorated in soothing blues, greens, and peach. Seeing her office made her feel better and guilty at the same time. Why did she always have to be nearby whenever a dead body turned up?

Harriet made straight for the seating arrangement and sank into one of the large, cushioned, rattan armchairs. She let out a hearty groan. Keeping up with three little girls for a full day had worn her out. She kicked off her trainers, set her feet on the low bamboo and glass coffee table, and closed her eyes. She'd give herself a few minutes to recover, then go see Alex and give him her statement.

"Harriet! Open up."

The sound of someone knocking on glass woke her. Harriet opened her eyes and saw that the sun's rays were slanted low through the French glass doors that opened onto a narrow lanai and the beach. She had slept much longer than planned. The dark outline of a man stood silhouetted against the left door.

Alex.

Harriet groaned and set her bare feet on the floor. She should have known that he would come looking for her when she didn't show up at the security office. Alex Hayes was nothing if not relentless.

"I'm coming," she grumbled. She yanked open the door and glared at the man she was pretty sure she loved. "I was coming by your office. I just needed to rest my eyes for a few minutes."

Amusement flared in Alex's deep blue eyes and the dimple in his right cheek appeared. "Don't tell me those three little lambs wore you out."

"Go ahead. Laugh. I had no idea kids could burn up so much energy. The first group wasn't like this. I swear those three little *lambs,* as you call them, have the energy of an entire barrel filled with monkeys."

She stepped back from the door and fluttered one hand. "You might as well come in."

She didn't want to let him in. She didn't want to see Alex at all. The fact that he knew things about her past that she didn't know herself made her feel exposed and vulnerable.

And it made her feel afraid. She felt afraid of what might be lurking back there in her childhood, else why did her aunt have her memory wiped?

As if he'd read her mind, Alex gently took hold of Harriet's shoulders and pulled her against his chest. He wrapped his arms around her and laid his cheek against her hair.

He'd missed her terribly. Being shut out of her life was not the reaction he and Payson had been expecting when they made the decision to try to help her regain her memories.

At first Harriet fought the urge to relax against Alex's broad chest, but eventually she relented and sagged against him. She had missed his smell. His voice. His strength. The rightness of being in his arms was too much to fight.

"Sweetheart," he murmured, tightening his arms. "I've missed you."

"I know." Harriet rolled her forehead against him, enjoying the feel of muscle beneath his polo. "I hate to admit it because I'm still upset with you, but I've missed you too."

She lifted her face so she could see his expression. "It's just that you laid that unexpected bomb on me and I can't even talk about it because every time I even try to think about those lost years I get a terrible headache. I don't know what to do."

She hated the pitiful whine in her voice. Even now she could feel a dull ache beginning to thud low in the back of her skull.

"I only want to help you recover what you've lost. It won't be easy, but I'm here for you. So is Payson."

"I'm barely thinking about it and the headache is already starting," she complained.

When Alex told her that the migraines she'd

suffered all her life were the result of blocks installed in her mind to prevent her from thinking about the past, Harriet hadn't believed him. Later she'd tested his words and found that he was right. Every time she tried to think about her parents, or dredge up a memory from her childhood, a pounding pain filled her head. The harder she tried to force the memory, the more searing the pain.

Alex placed his hand under Harriet's chin and forced her to look at him. "Shhh. Don't think about it now. Payson and I have a plan. Just trust us, okay? Trust us to help you. Trust us to take care of you."

Tears clogged Harriet's throat so she couldn't speak. No one had ever offered to take care of her before. Her aunt and uncle had taken her in and complained about being saddled with a young girl. She and Solomon had looked out for each other when they were teenagers, but that was different.

She nodded her head and looked for another subject that wasn't so fraught with pain and suffering.

"Would you like to take my statement now?"

Alex brushed a kiss against her forehead. "That's my girl. Yes, I would like to get your version of finding the dead man at the water slide–although I have a good idea of what happened from the two slide attendants. Still, I always like to get your take."

Harriet grabbed a couple tubes of water from her cooler unit and led Alex out onto the lanai. She plopped down onto the edge of the wooden platform and plunged her bare feet into the warm, fine sand.

The sun was nearly touching the horizon and had turned the ocean a brilliant blood red. Once it sank out of sight the island would be plunged into night. Unlike Maine, there was no long twilight, either at sunset or daybreak.

The gentle breeze carried the salty brine of sea air and ruffled her long hair. Several dark seal heads appeared close to shore, then disappeared beneath the waves.

A pair of guests, arms twined around each other's waists, stood at the water's edge watching the sun's descent. They made a romantic picture against the setting sun. Harriet thought briefly of grabbing her video camera but didn't want to get up.

"So. Tell me about the water slide." Alex sat down beside her, touching her from knee to shoulder.

She welcomed the feel of his warm body pressed against her own. Alex was solid. Dependable. Trustworthy. She took a few deep breaths and then began to relate everything she could remember about the water slide.

Alex asked a couple questions to clarify a few points and thanked her. Together they watched the sun sink below the horizon in a comfortable silence. When the last sliver of sun disappeared, the sky turned inky black. A thin crescent moon accompanied by a bright star hung high above the horizon.

Alex wrapped his arm around Harriet's shoulders and held her close. He brushed his lips across her temple.

"It's not a star," he said softly. "That's a planet. Venus."

Harriet hadn't realized she had spoken aloud. She felt content, she realized, better than she had felt since the meeting with Alex and Payson in Payson's cottage. She had reacted to the bombshell that her aunt and uncle had had her memory wiped the way a spoiled child would. It was time to act like an adult and accept their help.

Part of her desperately wanted to regain her memories of her parents. But another part of her was terrified of those memories and she didn't understand why.

A sharp stab of pain went through her head, the way it did every time she tried to remember her parents. Harriet forced her thoughts to the present.

"I'm sorry I've been avoiding you." She sighed. "I guess I owe Payson an apology as well. I know you're both only trying to help me. It was just so–so *unexpected,* you know?"

"I know. Let it go for tonight. Are you hungry? We can pick something up from the employee restaurant. Or I have bagels in my Redi-meal."

Harriet's link vibrated in her pocket. When she saw that it was Solly she answered with a smile.

Her friend squinted at her with a puzzled frown. "Where are you, Harry?"

"On my office lanai. Alex and I were just discussing what to do about dinner."

Solly smiled. "Hi, Alex. Why don't you two join me? I just scored a bunch of fresh scallops from one of the chefs. With a salad there's plenty for the three of us."

Harriet looked at Alex. "Definitely," he said.

"Great. No rush. I'll work on the salad and wait for you. And you can tell me all about the body you found today." Solly cut the link before Harriet could come up with a retort.

Alex laughed and squeezed her shoulder before letting her go. "You're developing quite a reputation, you know. I overheard a hotel employee refer to you as the Queen of the Dead today."

"Not funny," grumbled Harriet. "It's not my fault that people come here and find a way to get themselves killed."

"True." Alex pulled her to her feet and laid a light kiss on the bump on the bridge of her nose. "But somehow you always seem to get caught up in the thick of things. And you have to admit that you're always stumbling across the bodies. Go lock up. I'll meet you out front with a cart. I'd suggest a romantic walk along the beach to your place but you're so tired I'm afraid I'd have to carry you most of the way."

He disappeared around the corner of the building before Harriet could defend herself. It wasn't her fault that people kept getting murdered on the island.

At first Harriet had been afraid that the guests would cancel their reservations after word of the first death got out. She worried that the resort would fail before it really had a chance to get going.

A few guests did cancel, but far more reservations poured in. After the second death, and then the third and the fourth, they were turning callers away and were booked solid for the next two years with a waiting list. Turns out, people were ghouls. They loved the intrigue of murder as long as it didn't touch them.

That was a good thing, since Alex apparently had another murder on his hands.

CHAPTER FIVE

Ten short minutes later Alex parked the cart in front of Harriet's place. A round plaque with the picture of a mermaid sitting on a rock at the edge of the sea over the cottage door identified Mermaid cottage.

One of four employee cottages set near the southern end of the island, Mermaid cottage was far nicer than anywhere else Harriet had ever lived. Her dearest friend Solomon's Venus cottage sat next door. The remaining two cottages were empty at the moment. Most of the other resort employees lived in employee apartments closer to the hotel and restaurants. A few, like Alex and Chef Fritola, lived over their offices.

Alex took Harriet's hand and kissed her palm. He felt almost giddy with relief that she was speaking to him again. He had begun to fear that he and Payson had made a serious tactical blunder when they told her what her aunt had done to her memories.

But how else were they to start the process of repairing the damage? It wasn't something you could sneak by a person, like hiding a pill in a piece of cheese for a dog.

"Do you need anything from Mermaid?" he asked.

"Yes. Let me grab a bottle of wine from my chiller." She slipped her hand free and decoded the security lock on the front door. Alex had added the lock after a jealous stalker had tried to kill Harriet when she first arrived on the island.

The four cottages were nearly identical in layout and decor. Walls and ceilings were paneled in rich, red-brown mahogany. Woven grass mats dotted the pale bamboo floors and anchored a comfortable seating arrangement in the living room. A wall of floor to ceiling French doors in the living room and the bedroom looked out over the ocean.

At first Harriet had thought the cottage's dark mahogany paneling was too dark and would be depressing to live with, but after a week on the island she welcomed the cool and shadowed respite from the hot, tropical sun.

She dropped her backpack onto one of the deeply cushioned chairs in the living room and hurried into the kitchen. All four employee cottages were equipped with high end appliances in case the tenants felt like cooking. Harriet loved her pale rose granite counters and island. She didn't cook much herself, but she appreciated the beautiful kitchen. It too opened onto the lanai that ran the beachfront length of the cottage.

"Hurry up in there," Alex called from the front door. "I'm famished."

Harriet grabbed a bottle of chilled sauvignon blanc from her chiller and hurried back to Alex. "Here." She thrust the bottle into his hand. "Let's go."

The plaque over Solly's front door was a replica of Botticelli's 'Birth of Venus'. The lovely Venus's naked body, complete with modestly placed blond tresses, stood on a scallop shell floating on the waves. Both Mermaid's and Venus's bathrooms featured larger, more complete versions of their respective plaques done in mosaic and covering the bathrooms' vaulted ceilings.

The craftsmanship that went into building the employee cottages was just one example of the thought and expense Douglass Wade had put into his luxury resort. The same attention to detail and little extras could be found everywhere on the island.

"Solly, we're here!" Harriet called out as she pushed open the front door and entered Venus.

"In the kitchen! I hope you brought wine." Solly's head appeared in the opening that led to the kitchen. His lit up when he saw the bottle in Alex's hand. "Oh good. I forgot to order wine this week. Pour us all a glass, would you Alex?"

"*You* forgot wine? That isn't like you, Sol." Harriet led the way into Solly's kitchen. A large salad of mixed greens and deep orange mango slices filled a brightly decorated pottery bowl on Solly's gleaming black granite island. A platter of scallops waited on the counter next to the cook top. She slid onto a bar stool and smiled at her friend.

He shrugged. "It happens. I've been busy."

Island life agreed with Solly. His position with the resort required the handsome head gardener and groundskeeper to spend most of his time outside. The time in the sun had created highlights through his thick, sable brown hair and colored his complexion an attractive golden brown.

She inspected her best friend closely, trying not to let him see that she was looking for any lingering aftereffects of the terrible injury he had sustained. Unfortunately he knew her as well as she knew him.

"I'm *fine*, Harry." Solly pointed a long, two-pronged cooking fork at her. "Stop looking at me like that. I saw Dr. Clarke yesterday and she was very pleased with my recovery so you can stop worrying. *I'm fine*," he repeated.

Harriet twisted her lips in a rueful scowl. "Okay, okay. I can't help it. I almost lost you."

Solly turned back to the cooktop and ignited a burner under a fry pan. "It's nice to see you again, Alex." He shot a pointed look at Harriet. "We've missed you around here."

Alex pulled the cork from the chilled wine and poured three glasses. He handed one to Harriet and one to Solly and raised one. "It's nice to be back," he said mildly. "I've missed you both, too." He wasn't about to go into why he'd been banished the past week.

Harriet stepped over to the lanai door and looked out the window. She didn't want to discuss why they hadn't seen much of Alex recently since it was her fault.

"So, I found a body today, Solly." Maybe not the best alternative subject, but it popped out of her mouth before she could give it much thought.

Solly turned his head and flashed her a grin. His warm brown eyes sparkled with laughter. "So

I heard. You do have a knack for coming across dead people. Rumor has it that the other employees have nicknamed you the Queen of the Dead." He chuckled. "I about peed my pants laughing when I heard that one."

"It's not funny, Sol." Harriet scowled at her best friend over the rim of her wine glass. "It's not like I go looking for bodies, you know. They just keep turning up."

"Hmmm. So tell me about this one. Where'd you find it and what's the story?"

The kitchen filled with the smell of scallops frying in real butter as Harriet told Solly about the dead man popping out of the water slide. He laughed when she described Hayley's scowl because the body had made her lose the race down the slides.

Handing Harriet a small bowl and whisk, Solly told her to dress the salad. In a few short minutes they were seated on Solly's lanai with plates of food.

The perfectly cooked scallops tasted sweet and succulent. The crisp salad of bitter and sweet greens with the luscious mango in a bright, citrus dressing made a perfect accompaniment.

As she ate, the soothing atmosphere began to help ease the tension from Harriet's body. No one spoke while they enjoyed Solly's meal. Enough soft light spilled from the living room to eat by, eliminating the need for an outside light.

The crescent moon and Venus balanced on the horizon and would soon disappear. The sound of waves lapping softly at the sand and the buzz of night insects accompanied the occasional clink of a fork against a plate. The lanai smelled of salt breezes and the night-blooming jasmine Solly had growing in pots.

Harriet heaved a sigh. She was with the two people she loved most in the world. No matter how difficult it proved to be to face her past she knew Solly and Alex would be there for her. She scowled as the familiar dull ache began to pound in her head at the thought of her past.

She was ready to deal with it, she realized with surprise. More than ready. The knowledge that she could rid herself of the artificially induced migraines that she had accepted as a natural part of her life thrilled her.

The dull throbbing in Harriet's head intensified. A warning that it was time to think of something else.

"Were you able to identify the victim, Alex?" she asked as she set her empty plate on the deck at her feet and held out her glass for more wine.

"Yes." Alex poured the wine for Harriet and handed the bottle to Solly. "He was a resort employee–worked at the marina. A boat rigger, according to Leonard."

Leonard Dixon managed the resort's marina. An average looking man with beautiful brown bedroom eyes and an easy-going personality, the well liked and respected Leonard and his wife Dorinda had recently had a baby girl. Baby Rose could well be the most adorable baby Harriet had ever seen. She took advantage of the opportunity to hold and play with Rose whenever she happened to catch her visiting the marina with her mama.

"How did a marina mechanic end up dead in the water slide?" Solly asked. He stretched his long legs in front of him and leaned his head back to look at the stars.

"That's a very good question. Someone hit Frank Davis in the back of the head with a hard object, crushing his skull, and then stuffed him inside the slide. The reason the slide attendants didn't find him in the lagoon this morning was that he got hung up on a bend in the slide."

"Until Hayley came along and pushed him out," Harriet put in. "Poor kid."

"Hmmm. It sounds as if this Davis met his killer at the top of the slide, else the killer would have had to haul the body up the steps to the top." Solly rolled his head to the side and looked at Alex. He had helped Alex solve others murders on the island, something he rather enjoyed.

"Do you need somebody to help recreate the scene? If so I'm available," he offered.

"I'm going to take you up on that. Davis wasn't a very large man, but I agree with you–he most likely met his killer at the top of the slide."

"Davis?" Harriet frowned. "I overhead someone talking about a Davis today at the circus."

"Did you now? Who was this and what did they say?" Alex's tone sharpened like a hunting dog on point.

Harriet thought back to the conversation she'd overheard.

"I was dumping trash into a recycle bin between two food tents," she said slowly. "I couldn't see the speakers, and they were almost whispering, but they sounded like two men."

"They mentioned Frank Davis's name?"

"They were talking about *a* Davis. I never heard them say the name Frank, so they might not have been talking about the same man."

"I've checked the employee records and the current guest list. There's only one Davis on the island at the moment and he's an employee. What did they say?"

Harriet closed her eyes and pictured herself

standing between the two blue and white striped tents. The recycle bin had only been partly filled when she set the trash in it. It felt hot by the bin because the tents blocked any breeze. The voices had come from behind the tent to her left.

"The first speaker sounded angry," she said slowly. "I remember thinking at the time that he sounded mad about something. He told the second man that he should have left Davis to him. Then he made a comment about a map and three people making the search easier."

"Was that it?" Alex asked.

"No. Give me a moment. . . . The second man said that Davis was trying to cut him out and he'd been forced to do something about it. And then he said something about a diary. He 'had tracked down the diary,' that was it. The first man told him to quit throwing that in his face." Harriet shook her head. "That's all I remember."

"A map? Looking for something? Do you suppose we have treasure hunters on the island?" Solly frowned at Alex. "Have you heard anything about a treasure hidden on this island?"

"No. Can you go over what you heard again, please, Harriet? I want to record it this time."

Harriet repeated what she'd heard but had nothing new to add.

"All four coves with guest cottages are named

for pirates," Harriet pointed out. "And what about the sunken pirate ship in Black Bart's cove? It's proof that pirates visited the island. Maybe someone got it into their head that Black Bart hid treasure here. Pirates and buried treasure are a natural pairing."

"Good point." Alex steepled his fingers and tapped them together.

Harriet recognized the gesture as his deep thinking mode, a habit he had whenever he was trying to figure something out. She sat quietly, giving him time to work through whatever he was thinking.

Solly gathered up the empty plates and carried them inside. He came back out with three small white bowls of lemon gelato and handed them around.

"Yum." Harriet savored the sweet tartness of the creamy frozen treat. "Did you make this?"

"No. William is testing new desert recipes."

Harriet raised her eyebrows. "William? Who is William? Have I met him?"

"He's the new desert chef working under Chef Fritola," Solly answered offhandedly.

Too offhandedly. Harriet narrowed her eyes at her friend. "Is there something I should know about you and William?"

Solly ignored Harriet's question. He spooned gelato into his mouth and made a yummy noise.

Harriet's mouth dropped open. "Oh my god! You're seeing someone! *That's* what you meant about being busy. When did this happen? How did I miss it? You have to introduce me so I can see if I approve."

"And that's *exactly* why I haven't said anything," Solly muttered. He pointed his spoon at Harriet. "Leave it alone or I won't share any more of William's dessert experiments."

"Better do as he says, Harriet," Alex told her. "If William makes desserts like this you don't want to be cut off. I need to get back to my office and dig into Frank Davis. Walk me out?" He took Harriet's empty bowl and headed into the cottage.

Harriet stood to follow. "I'll be back in a minute," she told Solly.

"I can't wait."

Harriet ignored the sarcasm and hurried after Alex. He was already waiting for her in front of Venus. He clasped his hands on her shoulders and pulled her in for a hug. Wrapping his strong arms around her so she couldn't pull back, he buried his face in her thick honey blonde hair. She smelled of citrus and sandalwood and her own uniquely feminine scent, a scent he would recognize anywhere.

"Don't put up walls between us again," he said against her hair. "I can't bear it."

Harriet sighed and snuggled against him. She wrapped her arms around Alex's trim waist and pressed her lips to the vee at the base of his throat. She had missed his warm hugs.

"I'm sorry. But I can't promise I won't behave badly again. I don't know what I'm going to learn about myself and I have no idea how I'm going to react to what I do learn. Added to that, it upsets me that you know more about me than I do."

Alex lifted Harriet's chin with gentle fingers and brushed his lips across hers. "What I know, is that I want to marry you, Harriet. Your past doesn't matter to me. I love who you are now."

Harriet brought her arms up and wrapped them around Alex's neck. "I love you too. And if I forget to say it later, thank you for trying to help me." She threaded her fingers through his hair and tugged his head down for a long, lingering kiss.

"I have to go." Alex brushed another light kiss across her lips and stepped back. His white teeth flashed in the starlight. "Try not to torment Solly too badly. The guy's had a tough time of it lately. He deserves a little romance in his life."

"Oh, bah. If I can't torment him who will?"

Alex chuckled and climbed into the cart. Harriet waited until he'd driven out of sight before heading back inside Venus. She settled into the comfortable lounger next to Solly's and looked at her friend.

"Okay, spill. I want to know all about this Chef William."

Solly groaned and slid down in his seat.

CHAPTER SIX

Alex worked late into the night, quitting only when his eyes grew too bleary to read the reports on his screen. He stumbled upstairs to his apartment and fell into bed fully dressed. His alarm went off far too soon.

After a quick shower, he filled his go cup with hot black coffee and grabbed a bagel from his Redi-Meal and hit the road. His eyes felt gritty. Much as he hated to admit it, he could no longer get by on only four hours of sleep.

He was still a young man at thirty-two, but he'd spent too many of those thirty-two years running hard on practically no sleep while chasing murderers in New York City, until his life became little more than a succession of one grisly crime scene after another.

When he became a cop–and that was down to the fact that his eighteen year old sister had been killed because some punk ass kid wanted her new trainers–he had gravitated to Homicide thinking if he caught enough killers it would neutralize the pain in his heart over the loss of the one person he loved most.

The pain had lessened all right, but not because of the number of killers he had put behind bars. The pain lessened because of the passage of time, that great healer that helps people go on with their lives if they only give time a chance to dull their wounds.

He took several deep breaths of fresh, salty air and a sip of the dark, rich coffee and blessed the man who had seen fit to hire him away from a certain downward spiral.

Eventually the number of murder scenes he had attended and the killers he had put away only served to make Alex soul sick. He'd been close to complete burnout when Douglas Wade had called and offered him the position of security director for the resort.

By the time that call had come Alex had seen so many ugly crime scenes that they blended into one another and lost their ugliness. They became normal. He saw too many people hurting their loved ones because of greed or jealousy. He saw too many people willing to do grievous harm to the innocent over senseless things–like a pair of new trainers. Over time he had lost the ability to expect anything better from people.

"Crap."

He needed to shake off this morose mood and concentrate on the murder of Frank Davis. Despite an extensive online search that had kept him up until three in the morning, he hadn't been able to learn anything about the victim that would lead him to the man's killer.

It was early yet and the sun's rays had only just reached the peaks of the three mountains that created the backbone of the island. The golden rays caught the dew drops that coated most of the lush greenery lining both sides of the crushed shell road that led from the hotel complex to the marina.

Birds sang and squawked and lizards darted among the bright blossoms. A frilled lizard on the edge of the road flashed its bright red collar at Alex before slinking out of sight beneath the dense foliage.

Alex pulled the Road Hog into the marina's crushed shell parking lot and drank the last of his coffee while he inspected the boats and docks. A low, thin band of gray clouds clung to the horizon in the distance, marking an island that was little more than a big rock with a few shrubs jutting out of the water.

Set two thirds of the way up from the island's southern tip, the marina had been built for those who loved all things connected to the water. Its four main docks sprouted dozens of finger docks, all home to a wide variety of watercraft.

Sailboats ranging in size from single person sailing dinghies to large overnight cruisers that slept eight occupied one dock. Power boats for waterskiing, parasailing, fishing, sightseeing, and even two party pontoon boats were moored at the second of the larger docks.

Individual toys–florescent orange personal jet skies, kayaks, paddle boards and sailboards filled the two smaller docks. The bright orange made it easier to find any guests who might overestimate their abilities and find themselves in trouble.

The larger boats all carried tracking devices in their hulls that were monitored from the marina office for the same reason. So far the resort had not lost anybody, but Alex felt pretty confident the day would come. In his experience people could always be counted on to find a way to screw up.

Rigging on masts clanged quietly as the sailboats rocked gently in the small waves that slapped against their hulls. A speedboat came silently in to the docks. Like the resort's carts and the Road Hog, all of the boats ran silently on hydrogen reactors.

The only fossil fuel engine that intruded on the island's peace and quiet was Alex's Triumph Tiger. He had refused to accept the security director position unless he could bring his motorcycle with him. He'd spent three years restoring the lovely and powerful antique bike in his small NYC apartment. It was all that had kept him clinging to his sanity near the end of his career as a murder detective.

"Alex! Come in. I have Rosie with me so I can't leave the office just now." The marina manager beckoned Alex from the marina office doorway.

Leonard put a finger to his lips and lowered his voice. "Shhhh. She's sleeping."

Alex smiled and climbed out of the Hog. "Good to see you, Leonard." He peered closer at Leonard's face, saw the tired lines at the outer corners of his eyes and the purple shadows beneath and smiled.

"Rose still not sleeping through the night?" he asked sympathetically.

"No. The little devil is already cutting another tooth. I swear she purposely stays up all night and then sleeps during the day just to show me and Dorie who's boss."

Alex walked into the bright and airy office and went directly to the crib sitting beside the counter.

"She looks so peaceful," he whispered. The plump cheeked baby lay on her stomach and had one fist pressed to her mouth. Dark wispy hair haloed her tiny skull. One perfect, shell-shaped ear peeked through the dark curls.

A pang of longing took Alex by surprise. He wanted his own Rose. He wanted to experience what it was like to have a beautiful, defenseless baby depend on him. To love that baby without reservation. To help that baby grow into a decent adult.

He wanted a family. It had been just him alone for too many years. He straightened and stepped away from the crib.

"She's absolutely beautiful."

"Yeah. Yeah, she is." The pride in Leonard's voice was unmistakable. "Of course I can't take any credit–it was all my wife's doing. I brought Rose in with me this morning so Dorie could snatch a few winks. She'll be by around midday to pick her up."

Leonard touched his daughter's back gently, then rounded the counter and sat at one of two blue metal desks. He motioned to Alex to sit at the other before putting his feet up on his desk corner, obviously settling in for a chat.

"Have you been looking for a new assistant manager?" Alex asked, taking the offered seat at the currently empty desk. "It's been what, three months since you lost Whitfield?"

Leonard scowled. "About that long. I need someone who won't mind Rose being around. And someone who can let the superior airs some of our guests put on roll off their back. I don't want to make the same mistake I made with Ed so I'm being cautious, you know?"

"You might check with Payson Douglas. He seems to know a lot of people and he might have someone to recommend. He has a cottage on Kidd's Cove. I can have him call you if you'd like."

"That would be great. I can't not be here since I don't have anyone to cover for me, so the sooner I find an assistant manager the better. I could really use a day off to catch up on my sleep. Now what can I do for you? I know you didn't just stop by for a chat."

"Frank Davis."

Leonard's lips twisted in a half-grimace. "I heard. Harry found his body, didn't she? Frank was one of the people I was considering for the assistant manager position but there was something that held me back from offering him the job."

Alex's attention sharpened. This was the kind of information he always looked for. People's gut feelings about a victim often told him things about the deceased or suspects that he couldn't suss out in any other way.

"What kind of something held you back from offering Davis the job? He must have been a steady worker or you wouldn't have considered him for the position in the first place."

Leonard picked up a reel of fishing line he'd been about to load onto a spin rod while he considered Alex's question. After a long minute, he set the reel down and shrugged one shoulder.

"That's just it. I still can't put my finger on it. I never caught Frank at anything dishonest, but I always had the feeling he wasn't being entirely straight with me. His references all checked out when I hired him. One reason I took him on was because he was certified in scuba and could take out any resort guests who wanted to dive."

"Did he ever mention treasure hunting?"

Leonard blinked. "What, here on the island?"

"Anywhere at all. Did you ever hear him talk about it?"

"Nope. Why? Do you think he was hunting for treasure on the resort?"

“I don’t know what to think. I’m just collecting data at this point.”

Leonard shook his head. “I never heard Frank mention treasure. He frequently studied the charts for the island, but I assumed that was to identify the best scuba spots.”

Alex pushed his chair back and stood in one fluid motion. “Mind if I speak to Davis’s coworkers?”

“Not at all. The droids he worked with are all activated and down by the docks. Aron and Roberta should be cleaning up the pontoon boats. Apparently some of the guests had a little too much fun and lost their dinners last night.”

“Nice. Thanks, Leonard. I’ll talk to Payson and and ask him about getting you some help in the office.”

“Thanks for that. And don’t be such a stranger. The only time I see you is when you’re either rescuing someone or looking for a killer.”

Alex shut the office door quietly behind him so as not to wake the baby and headed for the docks. He’d talk to Aron and Roberta first, he decided, then the droids.

CHAPTER SEVEN

An onshore breeze had picked up while Alex was talking to Leonard, carrying with it the strong scent of salty brine and water. He took several deep, invigorating breaths. He loved the smell of the ocean. It smelled worlds better than the streets of NYC.

He spotted the two pontoon boats at the end of the power boat dock and headed that way. The wind blown waves had picked up, slapping loudly against the hulls and slurping underneath the weathered, silver gray boards of the docks.

Deep green fronds of seaweed undulated in the clear water. Large, pale orange starfish clung to the dock pilings and moved across the sea floor. White barnacles clinging to the dark pilings waved their feathery appendages searching for food. There was a whole world under the surface of the water, one that he had never explored.

He made a mental note to go back to Leonard and find out how often and where Frank Davis dove.

The gleaming white twin floats of the cheery pontoon boats contrasted nicely with the resort blue canvas curtain rails and bimini tops. White benches snugged up against the rails and wrapped around the perimeter of each deck, leaving the center of the decks clear–for dancing? General mingling? Alex had no idea what the guests did while slowly cruising around on a pontoon boat.

A wide swim platform hung off the rear of both boats, making him wonder if the boats were used for diving.

"Can I help you?"

A petite brunette with large hazel eyes and a wide smile greeted Alex from the deck of the left hand pontoon boat. She was on her knees, scrubbing the side of the pilot's console.

Alex flipped up a section of the side rail and stepped aboard.

"Are you Roberta? Leonard told me you and Aron were cleaning the party boats."

The brunette wrinkled her pert little nose. "I am Roberta, and I'm very sorry to say that I am indeed cleaning up after a party. What can I do for you?"

"My name is Alex Hayes. I'm the resort security director. I wonder if I could ask a few questions about one of your co-workers."

The smile disappeared. "I know who you are, Mr. Hayes. This is about Frank, isn't it? I heard that he was killed yesterday."

"Yes, this is about Frank Davis. How well did you know Mr. Davis?"

Roberta sat back on her heels and frowned. "Not very well. We didn't work together very often. I mostly work with the kids who want to learn how to sail or paddle board." She waved at the tote of cleaning supplies. "And I clean up after the guests have had their fun. Frank mostly either took out parties who wanted a fishing guide or guests who wanted to dive. I helped haul gear for him now and then."

Alex sat on one of the long side benches and stretched out his legs. The boat was comfortable. Not his cup of tea–he preferred speed boats–but he could see that it filled a niche.

"Have you worked here long?" he asked.

Roberta shrugged. "Since the marina opened. I like boats and I like people. I worked a marina in Boston but I hated winters. The resort is ideal. Year round work and top of the line watercraft."

"Did you ever dive with Frank Davis or talk to him about it?"

"No. Diving scares me. I prefer to stay on top of the water, not under it."

Alex asked a few more questions but didn't pick up anything useful. Roberta seemed honest and sincere. Nothing she said twigged his radar. He said his thanks and headed to the twin pontoon boat on the opposite side of the wide dock.

"Aron?" He didn't wait for an answer before stepping aboard.

Aron stopped hosing down the deck and frowned at Alex. "I haven't done anything wrong."

Interesting. Obviously the dock worker *had* done something wrong if he was issuing a denial before Alex had even asked him anything.

Alex took a seat and made himself comfortable. Spread his arms along the back of the seat and made himself look like he had settled in for a good long chat.

"Now, why would you assume that I'm here because you did something wrong?" he asked.

Aron had the look of a California surfer dude. Tanned, slim but well muscled, dressed in low slung colorful board shorts, a resort polo and boat moccasins with no socks. Shaggy blonde hair and bright blue eyes completed the picture.

Eyes that at that moment looked evasive.

Alex decided to press. "Aron? Things will go easier on you if you come clean."

"Shit. I knew it was too good to be true."

Keeping a poker face, Alex waited. Experience had taught him that when a person felt guilty about something they also almost always felt compelled to confess it.

"I knew it was risky, but I couldn't resist the extra dough, you know?"

"Whenever extra dough is involved there's often a price to pay." Alex was about to ask if this had anything to do with Frank Davis's murder when Aron tossed the sprayer to the deck in disgust.

"I don't see what's so wrong with giving some of the old broads a little pleasure in exchange for cash, you know? It was only the four. No, five. Who squealed? Nobody's getting hurt. The lonely hearts figure no one here knows them and their secret is safe with me. The gossips back home will never know they paid for sex on their little vacation."

Alex fought to keep the surprise from his face. Of all the illegal things Aron could have been up to, prostitution was not what he had expected.

"Aron, there are laws against unlicensed prostitution for a reason. You need to have a clean bill of health, pass mental aptitude exams. Etcetera. It's not just for your partner's protection, the licensing protects you as well. For all you know you could pick up an STD from one of your, ah, partners."

Aron ignored him. His mouth twisted. "Who snitched on me? The only mate I told was Dave. No one would ever offer to pay him for sex. He probably got jealous and decided to ruin my gig. Bastard." He spit over the side of the boat.

Alex had heard enough. "Dave never said a word. You snitched on yourself. I'm here to ask you about Frank Davis.."

"What? Well, shee-it." Aron plopped down on a bench. "That's just great. What are you going to do?"

Apparently Aron's attention didn't extend far beyond himself. The mention of Frank Davis hadn't even raised a blip on Aron's radar.

"Right now I want to ask you about Frank Davis," Alex repeated. "Did you have much interaction with him?"

Aron shrugged one broad shoulder. "Nah. Davis pretty much kept to himself while on the clock. He did a lot of diving and exploring the island during his free time so I never saw him. I was busy with other things. I don't think he spoke more than a few words to me. Mostly he'd just ask me to fill the scuba tanks and rig up a certain boat. He preferred to deal with Roberta."

"Did you ever hear him mention anything about a treasure? Or treasure hunting? Or a map?"

Aron's eyes widened with sudden interest. "Is that what old Frank was up to? Looking for buried treasure? Damn. He never said anything about it to me. Too bad. I'd have liked to get in on that gig."

Alex knew Aron had nothing more to give him. He stood to leave.

"Are you going to report me about the . . . you know?" Aron asked.

"Yes. I'm obligated to tell your boss. It's up to Leonard to handle it. If he let's you stay then you have to promise to quit your extracurricular activities. Every person here contributes to the resort's reputation. I don't think Mr. Wade would appreciate it if his resort becomes known as a sexual fantasy island. Get me?"

Aron looked relieved. "Yeah. Leonard's pretty cool. He might let me stay. And the pay is decent. I didn't go looking to become a prozzie, you know? I just fell into it when the first broad approached me."

Alex shook his head and jumped to the dock. He believed Aron. The boy simply hadn't been bright enough to turn down the extra dough for doing something that he in all likelihood would have done for free.

"Thanks for your time, Aron." He started toward shore.

"You might try that dude over at the circus," Aron called after him.

Alex whipped around and stepped back to the boat.

"What?"

"I saw Frank with a dude from the circus once. They seemed to be friendly."

"Do you know his name?"

Aron shrugged that shoulder again. "Nah. I'm not even sure I'd recognize the dude if I saw him again. It was pretty dark. They were sharing a beer on a bench in front of the hotel and I was jogging the beach. All I can tell you is he had dark hair."

"Why do you think he was with the circus?"

"He was wearing a red tank with the circus logo. You know–the ones reserved for the employees. They have shirts for the guests but they're different colors."

Alex probed Aron's memory for more detail but the dock worker had nothing more to share.

"Thanks, Aron. If you think of anything else give me a call." Alex pulled one of his cards with the security office number on it from his pocket and handed it to him. Aron took the card and slid it into a pocket.

"Sure. Hope I helped. Maybe you could put a good word in for me with Leonard when you talk to him."

"Maybe." Alex headed off again. He didn't have much, but he was beginning to build up a picture of the man known as Frank Davis. He'd talk to the droids next, then swing by the marina office and tell Leonard about Aron's extra money making activities before heading over to the circus.

He'd need help at the circus, he realized. He called Fox and asked him to meet him there in another hour.

CHAPTER EIGHT

"Harry, you've been avoiding me."

Harriet squirmed uncomfortably as Payson Douglas's pale blue eyes stared at her from her office link. She *had* been avoiding him–ever since Payson and Alex had told her that Aunt Wendolyn had had the memories from the years when her parents were alive erased.

Her eyes drifted to the cherry framed holo of her parents on the office bookshelf. She carried the holo with her between office and her cottage. It was all she had of her parents. If it wasn't for the holo she wouldn't even know what they looked like.

Her parents, frozen in a moment of happiness. Forever young. Her father stood behind her mother with his arms wrapped around her. They smiled out at Harriet, their expressions filled with love and promise.

She had found the holo hidden away in her aunt's attic and stolen it when she ran away. She didn't even know when or where it was taken.

She wanted her memories back. Except that there was something there, something deep and long buried that frightened her. And every time she looked at the holo or tried to remember her parents she suffered from headaches. The harder she tried to remember, the more debilitating the pain. Apparently all thanks to good old Aunt Wendolyn.

And didn't that just piss her off?

"Harry?"

Harriet pulled herself out of her reverie. "I'm sorry, Payson. You're absolutely right. I have been avoiding you."

Payson's eyes sparkled. "I'm surprised to hear you admit it. I missed our Thursday lunch. You can make it up to me by having dinner with me tonight. I'll pick you up at six-thirty." He cut the call before Harriet could find an excuse to say no.

She sighed and dropped the link on her desk. She had made up with Alex–she supposed she should reconcile with Payson too. After Solly and Alex, Payson was the most important person in her life, as much a loved, favorite uncle as a friend.

Payson apparently also had a tough streak she was only just beginning to experience.

Harriet grinned ruefully and returned to the paperwork on her desk. She continued to run regular ad campaigns even though the resort was booked to capacity for the next two years. They'd only been open three months and they'd already had five deaths. She felt that it was important to keep the positive PR going in an effort to counteract the bad publicity.

Not that the deaths had hurt business any, she mused, as she ran through the latest articles by travel writers and the comments on the resort's site by past guests. Apparently the old adage about any publicity was good publicity was true.

Cassandra Montgomery, the resort manager, had told Harriet that the murders would turn out to be another attraction. Much to Harriet's surprise (and a little dismay) Cassie had been on the mark. Calls for reservations had doubled after the last pair of murders.

What was it about unexpected deaths that engendered such morbid curiosity?

She would never understand the paying public.

And now they had another murder that needed to be solved. At least this time it was an employee murdered and not a guest. She'd take some comfort in that small blessing.

"Harry! You in there?"

"Just a minute, Cass."

Harriet padded across her office in bare feet and unlocked the door. A large body dressed in a flowing bright geen and lemon yellow caftan pushed by her. Despite her amply padded girth, the resort manager was light and graceful on her feet. She crossed the room and lowered herself into one of Harriet's large rattan armchairs.

Harriet followed Cassie across the room and paused by the cooler. "Lemonade?"

"Absolutely."

The kitchens delivered a pitcher of fresh lemonade to the offices daily, a perk that Harriet deeply appreciated. She poured two tall glasses and set them on the glass topped, bamboo coffee table before taking a seat in the soft cushioned chair next to Cassie.

Taking a long sip of the sweet-tart drink, she observed Cassie carefully. The resort manager's job was a demanding one and not made any easier by the series of murders, although Cassie waved them off as unimportant and good for business.

Harriet guessed her co-worker to be somewhere in her mid-fifties. She had pleasant features, warm brown eyes, and springy brown curls covering her head. She was pleasant to everyone unless she needed to get tough, and then she proved to be formidable.

Unlike Harriet's preference for soft, muted shades, Cassie preferred bright, vibrant colors and her office and wardrobe reflected her taste. She looked like a gaudy butterfly sitting in Harriet's pale peach cushioned chair.

Despite their differences in taste the two women got along very well.

Harriet smiled at her friend. "I wonder what brings you here?" She tapped her finger on the arm of her chair. "Let me think–it wouldn't have anything to do with the body I found yesterday, would it?"

Cassie pointed a be-ringed hand at her. "Got it in one. I swear you're better than a bloody cadaver dog. Do tell. I want the deets."

"Nothing to tell." Harriet shrugged one shoulder and set down her glass. She wasn't sure how much Alex wanted her to share so she erred on the side of not much.

"I was at the water slide with three of the orphans and the body popped out of one of the slides. I just happened to be there."

Cassie snorted. "You have a knack for 'just happened to be there'. Last time it was a guest who dropped dead at your feet." She gave Harriet a knowing look and leaned forward.

"What do you know about the latest body? And don't tell me nothing. I won't believe you."

Harriet sighed and gave up. Cassie wasn't a gossip. And as the resort's top employee responsible for everyone on the island she deserved to know what was going on.

"Fine," she grumbled. "The dead man's name is Frank Davis. He was an employee and he was definitely murdered. It looked like someone hit him on the back of the head. That's all I know."

Cassie squinted her eyes at Harriet. "All right. I'll be happy with that for now. Let's move on to the reason I'm here. I've hired someone to write some new scripts for our dinner theatre."

When Harriet had first devised a plan to revive the old murder mystery dinners from the previous century Cassie had fought her on the idea. Eventually she'd warmed to the concept and come to fully support it.

Recently Cassie had even suggested they name the program the Destination Death Dinner Theatre but Harriet had fought her on that, saying it sounded too tacky for a resort that was supposed to be the most exclusive vacation spot on the planet.

Harriet's mouth dropped open. "You hired

someone to write scripts? Isn't that . . . I mean, why would you do that? I found all those original scripts from the mid 1900s. They're working out fine."

Cassie gave what Harriet had come to think of as "The Look." Her delicate eyebrows rose and her head tilted slightly to the right.

"Those old scripts are too dated. We need stuff that is new and edgy. Her name is Fiona Sprite. And yes, before you ask, I suspect she changed her name. She arrived the same day as your orphans."

Harriet raised her eyebrows. "She's been here three days and you're just getting around to telling me now?"

"Yes. And before you get on my case about not telling you, keep in mind that you haven't been around much. First it was Solly in the hospital. Now your orphans are keeping you busy. Besides, I wanted Fiona to relax and get a taste of the island to help her with ideas."

"Okay." Harriet nodded. "When do I get to meet her? The mystery dinner theatre was my idea, you remember. I'd like to keep my hand in it."

"Absolutely. As it happens I've asked Fiona to put together a script about the first murder that took place here on the resort. She's been familiarizing herself with all the locations and talking to people. The plan is for her to interview you for your version of events, then she'll head back to her place on the mainland to write."

Harriet choked on her lemonade. She coughed and gasped for air, then glared at Cassie.

"The first murder? But that's–No. No, no, and, oh yeah–NO." The glass of lemonade slammed on the table with a sharp crack.

"Come on, Harry. The victim has no surviving family members to lodge a complaint and you have to admit that it was a truly twisted tale."

"It was twisted all right," Harriet muttered. "I'll think about it, but my gut tells me you'll be setting a bad precedent. People will start planning to come here to do their dirty deeds in the hopes that they'll be immortalized with a dinner theatre play. No. Bad idea. Very bad idea."

Harriet stood and stalked to the door. "I can't go along with it, Cass. Miss Sprite will have to come up with some modern plot ideas on her own. She can't use our murders." She opened the door. "I have to get to work, so if you don't mind . . . "

Cassie stood and grinned at her, not in the least perturbed about being asked to leave.

"Just think about it, Harry, that's all I ask,"

she said on her way out. “Fiona will be here for another week. Thanks for the lemonade.”

Harriet closed and locked the door behind her, cleaned up their dirty glasses, and went to stand at the french doors. Sunshine fractured into a billion shining mirrors on the blue-green water. Guests walked and swam and lounged on the beach.

She opened the doors so she could hear the waves lapping the white sand and the cries of the ever present gulls before returning to her desk.

Still fuming over Cassie’s visit, it took Harriet several tries to focus on the task at hand. She was editing a short video presentation she was putting together to entice potential sponsors for her orphan project. As usually happened when she got working on one of her projects, the rest of the world faded away.

She was deep into the editing when a familiar voice behind her made her jump.

“Dammit, Solly! Don’t sneak up on me like that.” Harriet tried to scowl at her best friend, but he saw right through her. He always had.

“Sorry.” Solly didn’t look at all sorry as he sauntered into her office after slipping off his sandy trainers. He was dressed for running, something he had only recently taken back up after a month long convalescence. Harriet tried to gauge how he was doing without letting Solly know she was checking him out, but he caught her.

"Stop inspecting me," he ordered, pointing a finger at her. "I know what you're thinking. I'm fine. I didn't push too hard. My heart is still beating."

"Thank the gods for that. Did you go in to the greenhouses today?"

Solly was the head grounds manager for the resort, hired a month before Harriet. He managed seven greenhouses that provided not only the fresh bouquets that graced rooms, cottages, and all of the resort's public areas, but also the fruit and vegetables that didn't grow naturally on the island for the resort's kitchens.

It was a big job, a demanding job for Solly and his crew of seven, but it was also the job he'd been born to do. Solly connected with anything that grew in soil or water. His thumb was so green that Harriet had once dubbed him the Plant Whisperer.

Solly pulled a tube of cold water from her cooler unit. He held one up for her but replaced it when she shook her head no.

"Yes. I worked this morning, then went back to my cottage for a nap, just like an old man. Happy?"

"I'm glad to hear you're smart enough to not push yourself too hard, too fast."

"I'm glad someone's happy," he grumbled. He wandered over to Harriet's rosewood desk and eyed the scene on the monitor. "So, what's new in the world of public relations? More orphan stuff?"

"Yes. I think we're ready to extend the program to include orphaned boys. I'm a little nervous about it though, to be honest. I'm worried they'll be harder to handle. The girls have been easy. I split them into five groups of four and there's no shortage of volunteers to chaperone them."

Solly grinned. "Young boys are for sure not as cute as little girls, and they'll definitely be more challenging, but I'm sure you'll have plenty of volunteers." He grabbed a cushioned chair and set it in front of her desk, then sprawled in it.

"So. The reason I'm here. I met a Fiona Sprite this morning. She wanted a tour of the greenhouse where we found Bradley's body and tried to interview me about it. Do you know anything about that?"

Harriet sighed and slumped back in her chair. "Cassie was just here. Apparently she hired Miss Sprite, whom I understand is a scriptwriter, to come up with some more modern scripts for our mystery dinner theatre."

The tube of water paused halfway to Solly's mouth. His eyebrows went up. "She's writing about murders at the resort?"

"Yes." Harriet scowled. "At least, Bradley's murder. And before you say anything, no, I'm not at all comfortable with that."

"Can't say I blame you. I put her off but she doesn't strike me as someone who will give up easily. What do you want me to do?"

"Avoid her, at least until I meet and talk with her. I'll try to track her down today."

"Roger that." Solly stood and made to leave. "Dinner tonight?"

"Can't. I'm having dinner with Payson."

"Ah."

Harriet cocked her head and narrowed her eyes. "What do you mean, 'Ah'?"

"Nothing. I assume you've forgiven Payson for–you know." Solly rolled his empty hand.

Harriet was well aware that Solly had been involved in the–she didn't know what else to call it other than an intervention–staged by Payson and Alex, even though he hadn't been there. Knowing that Solly was her closest friend and knew more about her than anyone, the other two men would have consulted with him.

Her link buzzed before she could pursue the matter with him.

"Yes." She didn't recognize the female face staring at her but she had a feeling she knew who it was. Her suspicions were immediately confirmed.

"Harriet Monroe? I'm Fiona Sprite. Cassie gave me your number. I wonder if you could spare me twenty minutes of your time before you quit work for the day?"

"Why not?" Harriet shot a glare at Solly. "I'm not getting anything done here anyway. I'll meet you on the beach in front of my office in fifteen minutes." She cut the call before Fiona could reply.

Solly gave her a bright smile. "Yes, well. I'd best be off then. Talk to you later." He was through the french doors and jogging south before Harriet could say anything.

"Coward!" she shouted after him. It didn't matter that Solly was one of the bravest men she knew. It felt good to be able to yell at someone and she knew he would take it and not hold it against her.

Harriet put away the project she'd been trying–unsuccessfully–to work on and locked up her office before heading to the beach to meet with Fiona Sprite.

CHAPTER NINE

Harriet removed her shoes and stood at the edge of the water while she waited for the scriptwriter to arrive, letting the gentle, warm waves wash over her feet. Every time a wave receded with a soft hiss she could feel it tug away sand from beneath her soles until she stood ankle deep in loose wet beach sand. It was a lovely feeling.

The stiffening onshore breeze felt equally warm and pleasant on her face. It smelled of the sea, the smell of home. She breathed deep and focused on releasing her tension.

"Hello. Are you Harriet?'

Harriet turned her head. Her first impression of Fiona Sprite was color. A woman with bright red hair dressed in pink bermuda shorts and a lime green tee shirt walked toward her. Mixed with the abundant freckles covering the woman's body, Harriet could see the telltale red sunburn of someone who rarely ventured outdoors.

Reluctantly freeing her feet from the sand, Harriet focused her attention on the scriptwriter.

"Yes, I'm Harriet. You must be Fiona Sprite. Lovely name. And lovely choker."

Harriet took a closer look at the two-inch wide choker circling Fiona's neck. Tiny seed beads in silver and navy blue had been strung together in an intricate design that reminded Harriet of Celtic knots.

Fiona's painted red lips lifted in a smile. She fingered the choker briefly. "Thank you. It's a favorite. You might even say it's my signature piece."

Up close, Harriet could see that the woman was well toned and freckled everywhere with dark, irregular shaped, reddish-brown spots that reminded her of the speckled cowrie shells she occasionally found on the beach.

"And thanks on the name." Fiona's grin widened. "I agonized for a year before I had it legally changed. Song Li just didn't seem like a good fit for a young Irish woman, you know what I mean?"

She waved a hand up and down her sturdy

body. "And Sprite was–well, I had to do it, didn't I? I'm not exactly petite."

Harriet wondered if the writer was a body builder. She'd done a public relations campaign once for a women's body building competition. It had been a real eye opener.

The women involved had been serious competitors. She'd learned that many took steroids to get an edge on their competition and learned to recognize the ones who used the enhancement drugs. Several of the users Harriet had interviewed for the campaign not only had great muscle tone, the steroids had given their voices a not unpleasant, deep, husky quality similar to Fiona's.

Despite her determination to remain cool toward the scriptwriter, Harriet found herself smiling. She couldn't help it. She'd always appreciated people who could poke fun at themselves and Fiona had certainly done that.

The woman was definitely no sprite. Only a few inches shorter than Harriet's own five-eleven, Fiona easily packed another thirty pounds of what looked like solid muscle on her frame.

Harriet lost the smile and became all business. She wasn't sold on Cassie's reasons for hiring a script writer, but she'd give Fiona a fair chance.

"So, Miss Sprite, what can I do for you?" Harriet turned and began walking slowly down the beach. Fiona fell into step beside her.

"Cassandra Montgomery hired me to knock out a few scripts for your mystery dinner theatre. I thought it would be fun to start with the very first murder on the island."

Harriet stopped walking and stared at her companion. She had expected the writer to use her imagination, not write scripts based on real, *recent* murders. She felt her face flush with anger.

"Fun? You thought it would be fun for me to see the murder of my fiancé turned into dinner theatre? If that's what you think then you have a warped sense of fun, Fiona Sprite. One I don't care for."

She resumed her walk at a little faster pace. All her pleasure in the day had fled.

"Sorry. I didn't realize that Bradley Higgins was your fiancé." Fiona cleared her throat. "Maybe fun wasn't the best choice of word."

"And here you're supposed to be a wordsmith." Harriet didn't try to hide her sarcasm. "Apparently your research didn't go very far if you missed the juiciest bit about Bradley's death."

"Crap. Let's start again, shall we? I am a script writer. Your resort manager feels that the murder plays you are currently putting on are too dated for the modern audience and she hired me to come up with some new ideas. She mentioned using the murder of your fiancé so I assumed you were onboard with that. I only took a cursory look at the news stories surrounding his death because I figured I'd get the real story here. I apologize for offending you."

Harriet took a deep breath and huffed it out. "Okay. Fine. I'm sorry I jumped on you. Cassie and I are not in agreement about portraying the resort murders in the murder dinner theatre. I think it will inspire certain people to make a point of committing their murders on the island so they'll be memorialized. The fifteen minutes of fame thing, you know?"

"Interesting theory. Can I point out that there will be people who intend to commit their dastardly deeds here no matter what the dinner theatre does?"

They walked in silence for several minutes. Harriet could feel that Fiona wanted to push the topic but she wisely kept silent.

"You wouldn't be able to write about any of the other murders here anyway," Harriet pointed out. "There are family members who would be hurt and possibly be angry enough to sue the resort. We can't take that risk."

"Okay. Resort murders are off the table, although I was led to believe that Bradley Higgins had no living relatives."

"No. Other than myself, Bradley was alone in the world." The fact still saddened Harriet. Even though she no longer felt any love for the man and deeply resented the way he had treated her, he had still been a human being.

Fiona waited, but Harriet didn't add anything. She had no intention of allowing Bradley's untimely death to get turned into entertainment. Nor did she want to discuss his death with a stranger.

"I think that it would be best if you used the old board game *Who Did It?* to base your scripts on. That way no relatives will be offended and we'll be safe from any law suits. You can take the old murder tropes and modernize them *anonymously*."

"If you're sure–"

"I'm sure. Are you familiar with the board game?"

"No, but it won't take me long to research it. Would it be all right if I floated a few ideas by you tomorrow?"

Harriet smiled, relieved that Fiona was willing to drop the idea of using resort murders for her scripts. "I'd like to work with you on this," she said. "Tell me a little about yourself.

How did you end up with the name Song Li for starters?"

Fiona's humorless laugh grated. "I was born to a druggie prostitute whose view of the world was somewhat warped, to say the least. She couldn't hang onto anything, let alone a young child. Apparently she loved all things Oriental and she thought Song Li sounded exotic. Eventually a neighbor called Child Services and they took me away and put me in an orphanage. I lived there until I turned sixteen, at which time I declared my right to be emancipated and I left."

"I'm sorry to hear that. I hope that it was a decently run orphanage."

Fiona shrugged and looked at Harriet. "I heard about what you're trying to do for the orphans here. Miss Montgomery told me about the program when she interviewed me. I have to tell you I think it's a big mistake."

Startled, Harriet came to an abrupt halt. "A mistake? Why on earth would you say that, especially when you know firsthand what these girls' lives are like?"

Fiona's expression turned fierce and angry so fast it made Harriet blink. Her green eyes sparked with anger and bored into Harriet's.

"All you're doing is teasing them with what they can't have." She waved a hand in the air.

"They'll spend a week here living in luxury with plenty of food and sunshine and fun. Then they'll return to the dismal reality of their lives. You're giving them false hope, Harriet. You're only tormenting them with a taste of what they'll never have. It's not only wrong, it's downright cruel. I would even go so far as to say that it's abusive."

It wasn't easy but Harriet managed to hang onto her temper.

"We don't just send them back to their orphanage and forget them, Miss Sprite," she said quietly. "An education fund is set up for each child. We're working on lining up volunteers for a mentorship program so every child has an adult who is committed to looking after their welfare from the time they leave here until they graduate college or trade school–and beyond if the individuals desire to keep in touch.

"It may not sound like much, but we're trying to better the lives of as many orphans as possible. I know the program isn't perfect–it's a work in progress. We're learning as we go what works and what doesn't. What's needed and when. At least we're trying. We're doing our best to make a difference."

"Sorry. Sorry." Fiona held up her hands, palm out. 'I didn't realize. I thought you just brought the orphans here for a week so you could tell the world what big hearts you have and then forgot about them. Corporate PR for the richest guy on the planet, you know? I apologize, Harriet. Please forgive my tirade."

Harriet turned back toward the offices and hotel. She didn't want to bring Fiona to her cottage and it was already in sight.

"Perhaps you'd like to spend some time with a few of the girls while you're here. I have a group of three I watch over in the mornings. You're welcome to join us tomorrow. I can't tell you what we'll be doing, I'm afraid. I let the girls choose whatever activities they feel like. This group seems partial to the amusement park, but they might want to try something else tomorrow."

"I'd like that. I need to familiarize myself with the resort anyway for my writing."

"Great. I meet up with my girls in the hotel lobby at nine. I'll see you then. Now if you'll excuse me I have things to tend to."

Harriet turned south again and walked back toward her cottage. When she looked over her shoulder she saw Fiona standing there, watching her.

She could understand the woman's anger. She suspected Fiona's orphanage experience had been a poor one. Hopefully spending time with the girls the next day would warm her to Harriet's program. Maybe she'd even volunteer to join the mentorship program.

Fiona had obviously made a life for herself as a writer. Harriet didn't know how successful she was at it, but she had to have built a decent career or Cassie wouldn't have hired her.

She disengaged the security alarm for Mermaid Cottage, let herself in, and reset the alarm. She needed a nap and a shower before Payson arrived to pick her up for dinner. Harriet was very fond of Payson, but she suspected that it was going to be a difficult evening.

He wouldn't be able to help himself. He wasn't the sort of man to let things slide. He would want to discuss her lost past and how to go about retrieving it. In all honesty, part of her was eager to get on with it. Unfortunately a bigger part was terrified of what she'd learn.

CHAPTER TEN

At six-thirty on the dot, Payson pulled up in front of Mermaid Cottage in one of the resort carts. Harriet had been watching for him and ran out before he could walk up to the door. She set her alarm and hurried to the cart.

She'd been unable to nap. She tried reminding herself repeatedly that this was Payson, a man very dear to her and until the previous week, someone she loved to spend time with, but despite the stern talking to she gave herself she still felt nervous about having dinner with him.

"You look lovely, my dear." Payson leaned over and kissed her cheek. "Is that a new dress?"

"No. It's one I bought when I had to replace my wardrobe. Alex picked it out." The rose-colored linen sheath skimmed her body. She loved its simple, yet chic sophistication and the color was a wonderful change from the dark shades she had worn when she lived in Maine.

"You look pretty dapper yourself." Payson always looked elegant, no matter if he wore khaki shorts or a cream-colored linen suit like the one he currently had on. The man simply oozed style and class.

Harriet settled into her seat and turned to Payson with a bright smile. "Where are we dining tonight? The hotel rooftop restaurant?"

"Not tonight." He swung the cart into a u-turn and headed north. "I thought we'd dine at my place. If that's all right with you."

"Oh." Harriet's already taut nerves jangled a little louder. She would have preferred to dine someplace public. Public meant the conversation would remain light and impersonal. The last time she'd been in Payson's cottage things had gotten very tense and uncomfortable. Her smile dimmed.

"Ah, sure. I hate to have you cook, though. Are you sure you wouldn't rather go out?"

Payson reached over and patted her knee. "Not to worry, Harry. I won't drop any bombshells on you tonight, okay?"

"Sorry. I guess I'm–" Harriet raised and lowered a hand. She laced her fingers together and set them in her lap to keep from wringing her hands.

"I don't know what I am, Payson. That was quite a shock you laid on me the last time I had dinner at your cottage, and to be honest? I'm still uncomfortable with the whole thing."

"I know," Payson answered quietly. "What was done to you when you were a child was beyond the pale. Alex and I tried to come up with a better way to break it to you but we couldn't think of one. The direct approach seemed the best way. We were wrong and I apologize."

Harriet heard the regret in his voice and shook her head. "No, you weren't wrong. There was no gentle way to tell me. But learning that someone had messed with my brain–it was just so unexpected, you know?"

"Let's change the subject, shall we, before one of your headaches sets in?"

"Yes." Grateful, Harriet heaved a sigh. "You heard about our most recent body?"

"Oh yes. I don't know how you do it. You must have some very messed up karma the way you keep turning up dead people."

Because it was said with a grin, Harriet knew Payson was teasing.

"Thanks a lot." She gradually relaxed as they

discussed Frank Davis's murder. It was hard to hang onto tension in such beautiful surroundings.

Payson turned the cart down the road that led to Kidd's Cove ten minutes later and parked beside his cottage at the far end. One of four coves named after pirate's

A close friend to the resort owner, Payson looked after the resort and reported any issues to Wade. In return he had his own permanent cottage, a large two bedroom affair set off from the other three guest cottages on the cove.

The jungle grew right up to the cottages and the edge of the cove's narrow white beach, giving the location a much different feel from Harriet's own Mermaid Cottage and the broader, open beach south of the hotel.

The sweet scent of night-blooming jasmine greeted Harriet as she climbed out of the cart. Payson liked to garden and had edged his lanai with pots filled with a variety of flowers and herbs. A light breeze blew across the quiet cove, rippling the trees reflected on its surface.

Each of the resort's four coves–Kidd's, Blackbeard's, Morgan's, and Black Bart's–held four guest cottages and were marked by different physical features. Black Bart's had an authentic, partially sunken pirate's ship, a draw for divers. Morgan's was an excellent choice for families with young children because of its wide beach and shallow water.

The middle hump of the three mountains that formed the spine of the island seemed to loom over Kidd's Cove, hemming it in with the sea. The cottages here were well-protected from tropical storms and favored by older guests looking for peace and quiet.

Payson held the door for Harriet and ushered her inside. While all the cottages had been furnished with the same standard of luxury found all through the resort, Payson had definitely added his own personal touches to his home.

A collection of carved masks, some up to a thousand years old, decorated all four walls of the spacious living room. The masks showed every human emotion possible along with a few unique masks that Harriet swore must have been alien inspired. A couple of the faces looked so fierce that Harriet found them too disturbing to look at.

Several hand-knotted, antique rugs in soft blues and creams were scattered around the room. Paper books, a rarity in a world where forests were now protected and strictly controlled, were scattered on every side table. Their subjects were as intriguing as the man who owned them: world history, archaeology, religious rituals, horticulture, natural history–they were a window into how far and wide her friend's interests ranged.

"Something smells delicious." Harriet accepted a glass of chilled white wine from Payson. "What's for dinner?"

"Cajun Mahi fish tacos. I've been dying to try them."

A man Harriet had never seen before popped out of the kitchen. He looked to be about Payson's age, only not as comfortable with it judging from the artfully dyed brown hair and the tautness around the eyes–a telltale sign of face work. He was slightly shorter than Harriet, beefy but not fat, with even, nondescript features. Someone easily overlooked on the street.

"I'm Edgar Bainbridge. You must be Harriet Monroe." He held out his hand.

Harriet transferred her wine glass and reluctantly shook the offered hand. It felt firm and dry in her grasp.

"I didn't realize there would be someone else . . I mean, I thought . . ." She flushed.

"Ed called after I'd invited you to dinner," Payson said smoothly. "He needed to discuss a few rather urgent things with me so I invited him to the island. I didn't want to cancel our dinner. I hope you don't mind."

"No! Of course not." Harriet's head bobbed up

and down. At least Payson wouldn't be able to talk about anything personal with his house guest there. She should be grateful to the man, but she still felt uneasy.

"So, Mr. Bainbridge, what do you do? Are you in the resort business?"

"God, no. I work in imaging, mapping actually. You'll have to excuse me, I don't want to overcook the fish." He turned on his heel and hurried back to the kitchen.

"Why don't we set the table?" Payson said. "It sounds as if dinner is about to be served."

Harriet didn't relax until halfway through her second glass of wine. The conversation jumped lightly from topic to topic; the orphans, fishing, life on a tropical island compared to living in Maine, the business climate in Miami where Edgar had his offices.

The fish tacos were excellent–spicy hot and perfectly cooked and served with a creamy garlic ranch dressing, chopped tomatoes, and crunchy shredded cabbage.

"Mmm. That was wonderful." Harriet reluctantly pushed her plate away. She had eaten more than she intended, partly from nerves and partly because the food was delicious. "I hate to stop eating, the tacos are so good. Thank you for cooking, Mr. Bainbridge."

"Ed, please. Coming back for seconds is all the thanks I need, I assure you. I have to admit my adventures in the kitchen aren't always so successful."

"Why don't we enjoy our dessert on the lanai?" Payson suggested. "You two go ahead and I'll bring it out."

Harriet groaned. "I don't think I left room for dessert."

"Sure you did. I scored some mango sorbet from our new pastry chef. It's light and fruity and just the antidote to the heat of the cajun tacos. I'll bring you a small bowl, promise."

"Fine. It sounds too good to pass up." Harriet followed Ed onto the lanai and settled into a cushioned chaise lounger across from him.

"So, earlier you said you map and image, Mr.–uh, Ed. Would that be imaging ruins underwater, or buried in sand, or cities overgrown with jungle?"

"Nope." Ed took a sip of his beer. "Nothing quite so romantic, I'm afraid. I map brains." He didn't notice the way Harriet stiffened and warmed to his subject.

"After studying nearly a quarter of a million brain scans we're finally confident that we can tie certain physical anomalies in the brain to conditions such as depression or dementia.

"It's a fascinating field and a promising one for treatment options. Instead of treating the symptoms–for example, prescribing mood elevators to treat depression–we can identify and treat the underlying physical issue."

"Yes, that does sound fascinating." Harriet glared at Payson when he came through the door with a tray holding three small white bowls of sorbet. She accepted an offered bowl and a spoon and took a moment to appreciate the beautiful deep orange color and the bright tang of frozen mango on her tongue.

"So, Payson. Edgar Bainbridge just happened to call you today after I agreed to have dinner with you. Did you think I wouldn't figure that out?" She raised an eyebrow at Payson, who didn't seem the least perturbed that he'd been found out. Damn the man.

Payson took the last bowl and settled onto the lounger next to Harriet's. "If I had told you someone else would be here would you have agreed to have dinner with me?"

"No."

"Right. I knew that, Harry. I apologize for the subterfuge but I wanted you to meet Ed. We're long-time acquaintances, I promise. He's also the best at what he does and we agreed that it should be the first step toward unraveling your problem."

"There's nothing to feel ashamed or embarrassed about," Ed pointed out. "Your brain has been physically altered. We need to see in what way and just how extensive the changes are before we can treat it. That's where my mapping process comes in."

Harriet savored another mouthful of the cool, sweet and fruity sorbet before answering. Strangely enough, no headache had begun to beat in the background. Apparently, as long as she didn't try to think about her parents, she'd be okay.

Her curiosity finally got the better of her.

"All right, *Doctor* Bainbridge, explain the process to me and what you'll be looking for." She caught Payson beaming at her from the corner of her eye and pointed her spoon at him.

"Don't think you're getting away with something here. I'll find a way to get back at you for being so sneaky."

"I can take it. The important thing is making you whole again."

Harriet harrumphed and returned her attention to Ed Bainbridge. "Now about that scan . . ."

CHAPTER ELEVEN

"Mizz Mun-row! Here we are!" Hayley waved and yelled at Harriet from across the hotel lobby, her mini-posse at her side.

Harriet winced and looked around to see if any of the guests were offended by the loud greeting but no one seemed to mind. She hurried across the lobby, dropped to her knees, and gave all three girls a hug.

"Good morning, Hayley. Good morning, Dorian. Good morning, Amber Lee. Don't you all look beautiful this morning?" The girls beamed at her.

One of the first things Harriet did when she locked in a group of orphans for a visit to the resort was to gather the necessary information to shop for and provide each girl with a selection of new clothes, sandals, and trainers to wear when they visited the island.

Harriet didn't do the shopping herself–she was the first to admit that she wasn't any good at it. Instead she had several willing volunteers who went to the mainland and chose the items for the girls.

The clothes weren't fancy. They were sturdy and practical so they could also be worn when the girls returned to the orphanage, but they were colorful and new, not the usual hand-me-downs the girls were used to wearing.

So far every girl had been more than pleased with her new outfits. They also received colorful fanny packs monogrammed with their first names.

Hayley twirled in her peach-colored sleeveless dress. The full skirt flared, revealing thin brown legs and the bathing suit underneath.

Harriet grinned. "I have to work this afternoon, but I can hang out with you girls this morning. I wonder . . ." she pretended to be deep in thought. "I wonder where you'd like to go today? A hike in the mountains? The mangrove swamp maybe? I hear there are big saltwater crocodiles in the swamp."

"The amusement park! The water slide!" All three girls jumped up and down.

Harriet grinned at them. "Color me surprised. All right, ladies, let's grab a cart and head to the park."

"Good morning. I hope I'm on time." Fiona came up behind the girls and gave Harriet an expectant look. "Will you introduce me to your friends?"

Harriet was surprised to feel a little resentment toward Fiona curl through her chest. She hated to admit it, but down deep she didn't want to share her time with the girls. Stifling a sigh, she pasted a smile on her face. She had invited the scriptwriter to join them, after all. Good manners prevailed.

"Good morning, Fiona. Girls, this is Miss Sprite. She's going to join us this morning. Fiona, this is Hayley, Amber Lee, and Dorian."

The girls chorused a quick hello and raced off to grab a cart.

"As you can see they're eager to get on with today's adventure. I'm glad you could join us."

Fiona fell into step beside Harriet as she headed after the girls. "Where are we going?"

"The amusement park. It's the girls' favorite. Have you been there yet?"

"Nope. Will you spend the whole morning there?"

"Probably." Harriet quickened her step when

she realized the girls had piled into a four-seat cart.

"We need a bigger cart," she told them, indicating Fiona. "There are five of us."

Hayley climbed out of the front seat and scrambled into the back. "That's okay, we can squoosh together. We like *this* cart."

The girls looked expectantly at Harriet. They were so small they easily fit shoulder to shoulder in the back seat. She smiled at them and climbed into the driver's seat.

"Aren't you clever? All right, Fiona, climb in. We're off to the amusement park."

Once in the park the girls decided they had to stop first for several rides on the merry-go-round before heading for the water slide. Hayley reacquainted herself with her lion, talking in its ear and patting its painted, carved mane.

Harriet decided to join them on the ride, choosing a tall giraffe for herself, while Fiona declined to ride and stood watching.

Although she had filmed the restored merry-go-round for an ad, Harriet had never ridden on it. Riding was different from watching others ride, she discovered. The animals were satiny smooth, their glossy surfaces reflecting the colored lights overhead. Their beautifully painted, expressive faces were filled with enough personality to make them real for anyone with an imagination.

Even at her age, Harriet could almost make-believe the animals were real. Their movement made it possible to get caught up in pretending she was actually riding a long-necked giraffe, undulating up and down as they went round and round.

When the merry-go-ground ground to a halt, Harriet slid off her mount with a thoughtful expression. She'd never really considered the power and magic of make-believe before. There'd been no opportunity for it in her life–or at least not in what she remembered of her life.

Afraid she might bring on a migraine, she quickly turned her thoughts back to the present.

"Let's go on the water slide now!" Hayley tugged at Harriet's hand, nearly pulling Harriet off balance.

"All right. I even wore my bathing suit today so I can go on the slide with you." Harriet had dressed with the intention of joining the girls in whatever activity they chose that morning, figuring it would help her better understand the attractions the resort offered.

She'd already made an unexpected discovery about the power of the imagination and had a hunch experiencing everything the resort had to offer would help her do a better job as PR director. She'd try everything–everything but the roller coaster, that was. Nothing could make her get on that.

"Nice merry-go-round." Fiona rejoined them. "Must have cost a pretty penny to restore."

"I wouldn't know. Braxton Holliday tracked down the animals and did the work. It took him years. Braxton manages the amusement park. We're headed to the water slide now."

Harriet turned away from Fiona.

"I hear the slide is quite spectacular–like everything else on the resort."

Was that a slight sneer she heard in Fiona's voice? Harriet considered defending the resort but then dismissed the thought. If Fiona carried a chip on her shoulder it wasn't Harriet's job to knock it off. She was there to have fun with her girls and that's what she intended to do. Let Fiona stew in her own resentment. Harriet had learned early on that there were always people better and worse off than she was. It was a fact of life and not worth getting her knickers in a twist over.

She smiled inwardly at the phrase "knickers in a twist". Did Tarbell know that one? She'd have to remember to ask him.

"Mizz Mun-row, let's go!"

The five of them traipsed through the park, the girls talking non-stop while Harriet listened with a smile. Had she ever been that enthusiastic about anything? Certainly not after her parents had died.

The year she lost her parents was the year she went to live with her aunt and uncle, Wendolyn and Arthur Wainwright, a dour, strict couple who refused to allow any mention of Harriet's parents in their presence.

Harriet remembered those years with her relatives as unrelentingly miserable. It saddened her to realize she might have been happier if she had ended up in an orphanage instead.

Harriet liked the park best first thing in the morning. It felt peaceful without the clack-clack-clack and rumble overhead of the teen guests' favored roller coaster. Bird song filled the air. They flitted on the ground searching for insects and small bits of dropped food from the previous night. Nothing went to waste on the island.

The resort guests had plenty of choices when it came to entertaining themselves, and depending on the blend of ages on the island, they could be widely spread along the island's west coast.

Despite there being few people in the park, Harriet's group ran into another group of three orphanage girls escorted by one of the hotel maids near the food court. The girls greeted each other with enthusiasm and the maid's girls decided the water slide sounded like a great idea. All six girls took off at a run with the three women on their heels.

When Harriet popped out of the path beside the slide's lagoon she saw Hayley leading the way and already near the top of the waterfall with Amber Lee and Dorian close on her heels. The maid's three girls brought up the rear, climbing the steps as fast as their stubby legs could carry them.

"Are you going to try the slide?" Harriet asked Rhonda the maid.

Rhonda shook her head. Short and round, with pale creamy skin and a pleasant face, the young maid rolled her bright turquoise eyes.

"No, Ms. Monroe, I think not. I'm afraid I'd get stuck in that tube, you know what I mean?' She flashed a smile and ran her hand over one ample hip.

Harriet smiled. "Call me Harry, please. I'm only Ms. Monroe to the guests and people I don't like. I think I'm going to brave it. Who knows? I might be too long to make it around the corners. If I don't pop out within a few minutes send someone in after me."

Rhonda waved her off with a chuckle as Harriet began climbing the steps. They were deep and shallow, she noted, easy for short little legs to safely negotiate. Sometimes Douglas Wade's attention to every little detail in his resort simply floored her. How did the man do it? How did he manage to anticipate every need?

She was halfway up the steps when her three little charges reached the top and headed down the slide. By leaning forward until she was almost laying on the steps above her, Harriet could watch their blurred bodies as they shot through the clear tubes behind and through the waterfall.

A minute later all three girls shot out of the slide into the lagoon with screams of delight. They moved away from the ends of the slides and the next group of three girls shot out.

All six girls immediately headed for the steps to do it again.

"I'd better get a move on." Harriet's long legs swiftly carried her the rest of the way to the top.

"Hi, I'm Harry Monroe." She stuck out her hand to the female attendant, a young woman with dark skin and a shaved head. The attendant gave Harriet a warm smile and shook her hand.

"Heather. I know who you are. I saw you here yesterday with the girls. Looks like you're living up to your reputation for finding bodies. You made me the center of attention last night with my friends." Her grin widened. "Thanks for that. Be sure to tuck your arms against your sides once you start down."

Harriet paused to look around her. The slide was located on a lower slope of the southernmost mountain–a foothill would be the more accurate term, she supposed.

Above them, the narrow stream tumbled down the mountain's side, a silver ribbon flashing now and then through the jungle. A small natural pool surrounded with lush greenery had backed up behind the waterfall. Harriet smelled Heather's coconut oil sunscreen, decomposing soil, and the heavy perfume of a bright red flower she couldn't name.

She could clearly see deep green moss covered stones beneath the pool's surface. Something glittered briefly, catching her eye. She frowned at Heather. "Do I see something in the water? There?" She pointed toward where she'd seen the glitter.

"There's a fine mesh screen across this section of the head of the waterfall to keep debris and animals out of the slide. Are you ready? Your girls are almost here."

Harriet looked at the steps and saw that her

charges had indeed almost caught up with her. She grinned at Heather.

"I'd better get a move on or I'll be mowed down. They love the water slide."

She sat down at the head of the center tube, pushed off and lay back with her arms crossed at her waist. The wet against her back and sides was a brief shock at first, but her attention was quickly diverted when she picked up speed.

Blue sky alternated with rock and bubbling water over her head as the slide wound through the waterfall. The surface was slick and smooth as glass, without a single seam. She barely had time to wonder how it had been constructed before she shot out the end and splashed beneath the surface of the sandy bottomed lagoon.

"Only one run?" Rhonda asked, as Harriet joined her and pulled her tank top and shorts on over her wet suit. "It looks pretty fast."

"It is fast. I can see why the girls love it. It's way better than the old burning hot metal slide we had at my school playground. Are you sure you won't give it a go? You won't get stuck, I promise. The tubes are generously sized. I'll be happy to keep an eye on all the girls while you try it."

"I'll give it a shot, even though I don't have a suit."

Harriet jerked, and immediately felt embarrassed that she'd forgotten about Fiona. She turned around and forced a smile. "It's great fun. I'm glad I tried it."

Fiona headed up the steps behind the girls. Harriet saw Hayley stop and dig at something beside the steps halfway up the slide.

"Hayley!" Harriet called up. "Don't mess with the plants. You'll damage them."

Hayley ignored her warning. She seemed to be trying to get at something beneath one of the small ferns that flourished in the waterfall's fine mist.

"Hayley!" Harriet started up the steps and stopped just below where Hayley still knelt, her butt in the air and her head hidden by the ferns. The other girls and Fiona had continued past her and watched from the top.

"Hayley, what are you doing?"

"I saw some trash and I wanted to pick it up."

"Good girl. I'm proud of you." Harriet had been talking to the girls about littering whenever they were together. She made a point of getting them to pick up trash whenever they spied any and praised them whenever they did. Apparently her lessons on not trashing the planet were sinking in at least a little bit.

Hayley backed out of the ferns and sat on the step. She smoothed the piece of paper on her lap.

"Look, Mizz Mun-row. It's not trash. I found a treasure map." Hayley held up the creased, soiled piece of paper.

Harriet took the paper and sat beside the little girl. The last thing she wanted to do was to squash the little girl's active imagination.

"Let's see," she said, and carefully examined the paper. Expecting to see someone's dropped shopping list or office memo, she was surprised to see that the paper did indeed show a map. It had also been covered in a super thin laminate that was smeared with dirt and what looked like soot. The laminate explained why it wasn't soggy from the waterfall's spray.

"Wow, Hayley." Harriet put her arm around the girl's shoulders and gently squeezed. "You definitely found a map. It looks old."

"It's a treasure map," Hayley repeated solemnly.

Harriet smoothed the stained map on her knee with her free hand and examined it. It looked like someone had crudely drawn a map of an island and then somehow aged the paper. It had creases and thin spots, as if it had been folded and re-folded many times. One edge was ragged. The torn edge could only mean that at one time there had been more to the map.

She knew there were techniques used by con men to make a document look old. Without an expert's opinion there was no way to tell if the map was truly old or a forgery. Harriet suspected the latter.

"Why do you think it's a treasure map?" she asked the girl.

Hayley took the map from Harriet's knee and carefully folded it back up. It was obvious she had no intention of parting with "her" treasure map.

"Why else would someone draw a map of an island?" Hayley answered matter-of-factly. The kid had a point.

"Hayley, are you coming?" Dorian shouted down from the top of the waterfall where she waited with Amber Lee. Fiona stood behind them.

"No!" Hayley shouted. She waved the folded paper in her hands. "I found a treasure map!" She turned to Harriet and lowered her voice.

"I bet a pirate lost it. I'm going to put it in my fanny pack and keep it safe until he comes back."

Harriet suspected some kid had picked up the fake map somewhere and dropped it at the water slide but she wasn't going to poke any holes in Hayley's vivid imagination. Imagination was important. Imagination could carry a person through difficult times.

"Good idea," she told the girl. "After the others finish their slide let's get some lunch. I'm starving."

"Yeah!' Hayley jumped to feet and scurried down the stairs so fast Harriet was afraid she was going to fall. When Hayley reached the bench where they'd left their clothes she placed her treasure map inside her fanny pack and zipped it securely, pulled her dress on over her bathing suit, then put the pack on.

Dorian and Amber Lee and Fiona popped out of the slides and joined them. They took their leave of Rhonda and her three charges and headed for the food court.

Once settled with their meal at a picnic table in the shade, Hayley pulled her map out while they ate and showed it to everyone.

"Can I see it?" Fiona asked. Hayley held out the map but wouldn't let Fiona take it for a closer look.

"It's mine," Hayley explained, securing the map in her fanny pack. "Finders keepers rule."

Fiona frowned and tried to talk Hayley into letting her see the map but Hayley held firm. Harriet tried to squelch the petty satisfaction she felt.

Hayley had trusted *her* enough to show her the map.

The girls entertained Harriet with their plans to find the pirate who owned the map. When they found him they would ask him if they could tag along with him while he dug up his buried loot.

"If this is a genuine map you do realize that the pirate has been dead for a long time, right? That map could have been hidden beside the waterfall for years." Harriet saw no reason to point out that the laminate on the map was a fairly recent invention. Let the girls have their fun.

When they finished lunch Harriet handed the girls off to one of the spa workers for the afternoon. As much as she enjoyed looking after them she still needed to put in some work hours in her office.

The spa worker loaded them into a cart and the group, including Fiona, headed off to the circus to see Hayley's lions. Harriet grabbed a free cart and headed south to her office.

She was halfway there before she remembered something else about the argument she'd overheard the previous day at the circus. The man had mentioned a map, hadn't he? He had one half and the murdered man supposedly had the other half. She'd forgotten about that when she had related the conversation to Alex.

Telling Alex about the map could wait, she decided. The map was safe with Hayley for the moment and she really needed to get to the office. She'd call Alex after work and tell him about the map and the remembered snippet of conversation. Maybe he'd have some news about his investigation into Frank Davis's murder.

CHAPTER TWELVE

Despite the pressing need to pursue the Frank Davis murder inquiry, Alex and Fox didn't get to interview the circus folk until late in the afternoon. While tracking down a murderer as quickly as possible was important–and no one knew that better than Alex–he had other responsibilities for the resort that took precedence. Responsibilities the guests considered every bit as pressing as a murder investigation and maybe even more so.

When something didn't personally affect a person it was easy to ignore others' troubles.

There were the three teenage boys who'd taken out jet skis and failed to return. Thanks to one of the marina's speedboats, the tracking devices Alex had insisted on installing in each jet ski, and an aerial surveillance drone, Alex found them floating offshore near a mostly submerged island known to the locals as Halfway Rock.

Boys being boys–which usually meant they did things that were decidedly stupid–these three friends had dared one another to see who could go the farthest on a single fill up with no thought of how they were going to get back.

Sunburn wasn't the only explanation for the teens' red faces as they were towed back to the resort where angry and relieved parents greeted them.

Alex handed the boys over without a reprimand, confident that they'd learned their lesson. They would go on to do more stupid things–they were teenagers after all–but they wouldn't repeat that particular stupid stunt. Since no one had been hurt he called that a win.

After putting things to rights at the marina, he and Fox were called to the hotel where a distraught female guest loudly insisted that one of the maids had stolen her diamond necklace and earrings. After interviewing the understandably upset maid–who insisted she hadn't even *seen* the missing diamonds let alone made off with them–the woman's husband showed up.

Alex braced himself for trouble. He fully expected the husband, a highly paid CEO of a tech company, to make trouble for the resort. By this time the hotel lobby had filled with concerned and curious guests–not a good thing. The guests murmured among themselves, speculating about the maid's guilt.

The husband calmed his hysterical and nearly incoherent wife, but once he understood what the problem was he immediately upset her again when he yelled at her. *He* had taken the diamonds that she had so carelessly left lying around their suite and had them locked in the hotel safe. He apologized to the maid and gave her a large tip, apologized to Alex and Fox for wasting their time, and was yelling at his wife again when he ushered her from the lobby.

Another red face, another problem dealt with.

Alex jerked his head at Fox and made a beeline for the lobby's double doors. "Let's get out of here. I want to check out the circus before any other disasters happen."

Fox scratched his ear. "Well, wasn't that just jiggity-boo. The poor maid. I thought married people talked to one another."

"Don't ask me. I never made the leap."

Both men reached for their sunglasses as they left the hotel's cool, dim lobby and stepped into the bright sunshine. Ten minutes later Alex parked their cart at the circus gate.

"Hi, Tamara." Fox pulled his glasses down his

nose and winked at the circus's gate keeper. "You're looking *especially* fine today."

Tamara's bright green eyes sparkled. "Not looking too shabby yourself, Tarbell. When are you going to buy me that drink you promised me?"

"He'll have to get back to you on that, Tamara," Alex said, not unkindly. "We're working at the moment."

It hadn't taken him long to learn that his right hand man was an inveterate flirt. A burly Irishman with dark red hair, green eyes, a charming smile and a smooth tongue, Fox never lacked for female companionship even on the island.

What really impressed Alex was that Fox somehow managed to keep them all happy. When asked about it, Fox explained that he treated the women well and promised only friendship, making sure up front that he wasn't looking for a happily ever after.

Fox shrugged at Tamara now and raised his hands, palms up. "You heard what the boss said. Gotta go. As soon as we've figured out who washed away our latest dead guy I'll swing by and we'll set something up. I promise."

Tamara pointed a finger at Fox's chest. "I'll hold you to that. If you even *think* about reneging

I should warn you that my Uncle Sugo will sic his lions on you if I ask him. Just saying."

Fox hustled to catch up with Alex who was already through the gate.

"Did you know that the lion tamer is Tamara's uncle? I do believe the lovely gatekeeper just threatened me with bodily harm by lion if I don't call her." Fox grinned, apparently unconcerned with the threat.

"Everyone who works the circus considers themselves related in one way or another. I thought you knew that."

"Nope. I did not know that." Fox looked around. "Okay. What are we looking for?"

"Beats me. Our only lead–and it's a very slim, possibly inaccurate one–is that one of the marina workers saw our dead guy talking to a man he thought was with the circus."

"How did he know the guy was with the circus?"

"Apparently he was wearing an Angel Brother's Circus shirt. And before you ask, I checked. Only employees of the circus wear the shirt Aron described. The ones we sell to the guests for souvenirs are different."

"Okay. I'll take your word for it. Do we have a description of the guy?"

"Nope."

A stilt walker came striding toward them dressed in red and white striped pants and a red with white polkadot shirt. He tipped his high hat at them.

"Good morning, gentlemen. Welcome to the Angel Brother's Circus. My name is Lino. Is this a friendly visit or business?"

So, the stilt walker knew who they were. Alex wondered if Tamara had alerted the family that he and Fox were there.

"Business," Alex replied. "You could answer a question for me. Did you know Frank Davis?"

Lino stepped gracefully back and forth to keep his balance and furrowed his thick dark eyebrows. "I don't think so. I'd have to see his face to know for sure. Is that the fella who drowned on the water slide?"

"He didn't drown." Alex slid Frank's employment photo from his pocket and handed it up to Lino.

Lino took a good look and handed the photo back. "Never saw him before. If you'll excuse me I need to greet some more guests." He took off, his long strides eating up the ground.

"Lino must have a pretty good view of things from up there," Fox observed. "I'm willing to bet that he doesn't miss much that's happening around the circus."

Alex looked after the stilt walker thoughtfully. "We'll keep an eye on him. In the meantime, let's introduce ourselves to the rest of the circus folk."

They stopped at each food and game cabana and spoke with the workers, most of whom were temporary hires for the circus's off season. Alex showed them the dead man's photo, but no one admitted to knowing Frank Davis.

"Holy crap is this good."

Alex had to agree. They had stopped to try a piece of sugar-topped fried dough with a coffee. The dough was light and airy and tasted of cinnamon and sugar. Bliss on his tongue. Better than anything he could get in New York.

When he dumped their trash in a bin he looked at the tents on either side and wondered which bin Harriet had been using when she overheard the conversation about Davis. He made a mental note to ask her. Killers weren't always intelligent, especially when the kill had been impulsive. The solution might be as simple as identifying who worked the tents next to Harriet's trash bin.

"Shall we try Madame Zaza next?" Fox asked as they neared the fortune teller's tent.

"Sure, why not?"

The painted sign outside the small red and white striped tent showed a woman wrapped in a colorful shawl with long dark hair snaking over her shoulders. She held a crystal ball filled with swirling smoke.

"The Madame really freaked Harry out a few months ago when she told Harry's fortune," Fox said quietly. "Harry didn't want it told, but Madame Zaza insisted. I have to admit it was a strange experience. Freaked me out a little, to be honest."

Alex looked at Fox curiously. "You believe in that stuff?"

Fox snorted. "I'm Irish, remember? We have wee faeries and all sorts of magical folk. I know there are plenty of charlatans out there, but Madama Zaza–" He hesitated. "Well, let me just say that there's something about her that you can't brush off as simple showmanship."

"Right."

Alex pushed through the tent flap. He wasn't sure what he had expected to find, but the interior exceeded his expectations. Lit only by three tall pillar candles, the walls were draped in rich, colorful tapestries depicting the heavens and what he guessed were occult symbols.

Madame Zaza looked like her portrait on the sign. She wore a gold turban, long flowing robes, and the colorful shawl from the portrait, with silver bangles and rings on her arms and fingers.

Where the portrait failed was in depicting the power in Madame Zaza's dark eyes. They appeared to be fathomless, dark pools of secret knowledge.

Alex shook off the fanciful thought and introduced himself and Fox.

"I remember Mr. Fox," Madame Zaza answered, in a pleasant, husky voice. "He was here with the lovely young Miss Harriet. What can I do for you, Detective?"

"Just Alex will do. I'm no longer a detective. We were told that this man was seen speaking with someone from the circus and we're trying to locate that person."

Madame Zaza touched the photo lightly and drew back. "This man met with a violent end."

"Yes. What do you know about that? Have you seen him before?"

"No." She touched the photo again. Her gaze became unfixed. "I see this man near a waterfall. It is night. Very dark. He is meeting someone. A woman. No–a man. He's . . . angry with the man. Frustrated. They argue. This man"–she tapped the photo of Davis–"turns to leave and the other man picks up a rock and hits him on the head."

Alex pocketed Frank's picture. "Can you describe the other man?" he asked. Could it be this easy? Of course, if the fortune teller described the other man he could only assume that Madame Zaza knew the murderer and might be involved.

Madame Zaza jerked her head no. "He is no more than a dark shadow. I only know that your killer is a man. They want something. Something . . . something they believe is here on the island."

"Is that all you can tell me?"

"Yes. The gift of sight is not always as straight forward as some would like."

Disappointed but not surprised, Alex turned to go. "Thank you for your time, Madame Zaza."

Even with his sunglasses on, the sun felt blinding compared to the shadowed interior of the fortune teller's tent. Alex stood outside the entrance and took a deep breath while his eyes adjusted.

"Do you think Madame Zaza really saw Frank's murder?" Fox asked beside him. "Other than seeing a woman and then changing her mind, she sounded pretty sure of herself."

Alex shook his head. He didn't believe in fortune tellers as a general rule, but Fox had a point. Madame Zaza had not only seemed very sure of what she saw, what she told them matched the evidence they had gathered so far.

Also, her "vision" correlated with Harriet's overheard conversation between two men.

"We haven't made public any details about

how Frank Davis was killed," Alex answered slowly. "We've let everyone assume he drowned. She certainly could have heard that he was found at the water slide. News travels fast here. As for the rest of it? Madame Zaza certainly nailed the head wound. And a meeting would explain Davis's presence in the amusement park."

He shrugged. "It's a pretty safe bet that everyone wants something. She wasn't telling us anything new there. Let's finish meeting the rest of the Angel family and see if we turn up anything concrete."

The afternoon wore on. The sun dipped low on the horizon, its light warm and buttery. The lights and music gave the circus a festive air that the harsh tropical sun washed out during the mid day.

Like fairs, circuses really belonged in the colder northern European countries, Alex mused, as they walked to the main tent. Countries with twilight and early sunsets so the circus lights showed to dramatic advantage. Still, it made sense for the performers to have a winter camp to rest and work out new acts.

The resort was perfect for that. The small number of people wandering the circus grounds gave the performers feedback on the new acts. At the same time the guests knew the performers were on a hiatus and therefore they didn't expect a full blown show.

"So this is Sugo." Fox had stopped in front of a painted display showing a middle-aged, green-eyed man flanked by two lions.

Fox frowned at the sign. "I think I'd better see to taking Tamara for that drink. I'd just as soon skip a mauling by lion. Those teeth and claws look lethal."

The main tent was a giant version of the fortune tellers tent, red and white striped with a long blue banner flying from its center peak. They stepped inside and looked around. Short bleachers had been set up on two sides of the single ring.

A petite woman with flowing black hair was doing a handstand on the back of a cantering white horse. The pair circled the ring once. Alex watched, speechless, as the woman spread her legs in a wide split and supported herself on one hand.

"I couldn't do that on solid ground, let alone on the back of a moving horse," Fox said in his ear. "Wow. And she's beautiful to boot."

"Remember the lions, Fox."

"Right. Big teeth."

The woman gracefully flipped into a seated position on the horse's back and came to a stop in the middle of the ring.

"That looked great, Ellie. How did it feel?" called a voice from the back shadows.

"Good. I think Peg would be more comfortable if I moved a few inches farther back. I felt him tighten when I went to one hand."

"We'll fine tune it tomorrow. You've both done enough work for today."

Alex stepped forward and spoke before the rider could leave.

"Excuse me. Could I have a brief word? I'm Alex Hayes, the resort's security director. This is my assistant, Tarbell Fox. Beautiful horse you have there. We were quite impressed with your skill. It must take ages to learn how to ride like that."

The woman nodded at him and slid gracefully from the horse's back. Her green skinsuit clung to her small but sleekly muscled body.

"I'm Eleanor Angel. I'm pleased to meet you both, I'm sure." She ran her hand down her horse's neck and left it there. The horse nuzzled her, then stood quietly without a bridle or a lead.

"Eleanor Angel. How fitting. You ride like an angel." Fox gave her his most charming smile.

"My wife does ride like an angel." An equally well muscled man in tights and an Angel Brother's Circus red tee shirt approached them from the rear exit and stood next to the woman. He put a possessive arm around her shoulders and put out the opposite hand.

"Simon Angel. Eleanor and I do the horse act. We've been working on this new trick. Wait until you see the whole thing put together."

Alex hid his grin as he felt Fox deflate beside him. "I look forward to that." He pulled out Frank Davis's photo and handed it to Simon.

"Do either of you know this man, or have you seen him with anyone from the circus?"

Simon took the photo from Alex and showed it to his wife.

"Sure," he said, handing the photo back. "That's Frank Davis. Elle and I took a scuba diving lesson from him when we first arrived on the island. We figured we should take advantage of the warm water and learn to dive so we can enjoy the reef while we're here. Even though we're still working on our acts most days we try to treat the off season like a vacation whenever we can."

"Did you ever see anyone else from the circus with Davis? Or see him with anyone at all?" Fox asked.

"We only saw him the one time he took us diving. We met him at the marina. He took us to dive the wreck in Black Bart's cove. Coolest thing I ever did."

It was interesting how one man's cool was another man's ho-hum, Alex mused. Personally, he thought doing acrobatic tricks on the back of a moving horse was one of the coolest things he'd ever seen.

"I saw him with the woman who works for the marina," Eleanor put in. She shrugged. "But they work together so you would expect that, right?"

Alex tucked the photo away. "Thanks for your time. I'd love to see your whole act sometime. What little I saw was damned impressive."

"We plan to put on a full show for the resort employees before we head back on tour," Eleanor said. "We like to make sure it all flows. Be sure and catch us then."

"We will. Thanks again." Alex led the way out of the tent and stood in thought. Night was fast approaching. They still had at least a dozen people left to interview. His stomach was rumbling and he needed to check in with his office droid, Mary.

"Let's take a dinner break and come back," he told Fox. "There will be more people about, but we've already done the concession cabanas so we won't be in their way. We can catch the others when they aren't performing. I'll grab the list of circus employees from the office and cross off the ones we've spoken with–see who we have left."

"Sounds good. Why don't I meet you at the gate? If Tamara's free after work I think I'll take her for that drink. You know . . . lions, teeth, claws . . ."

Alex grinned. Tamara had chosen her threat wisely. He checked his watch "It's six now. We'll meet by the gate at eight."

He left Fox at the gate talking with Tamara and grabbed a cart.

CHAPTER THIRTEEN

Instead of heading straight back to the security office, Alex drove toward the southern tip of the island and Harriet's Mermaid Cottage. He had to laugh at himself when he realized what he'd done. Even though he hadn't consciously been thinking of Harriet, obviously part of him was focused on her.

He suspected that it always would be.

The sun was barely hovering above the watery horizon, casting a bright orange-red path on the surface of the turquoise sea. A trio of sleek dark seal heads popped up near shore and disappeared again, chasing a school of fish that had foolishly let themselves get caught near the shallows.

He breathed deep of the fresh sea air and willed the tension to leave his body as he released the breath. There was a killer on the island–again!–and it was up to him to discover who it was.

He had always treated tracking down a murderer seriously, but somehow it felt even more so on the resort island. Maybe because there were far fewer suspects. Maybe because the island had become his home, the other employees part of his new extended family.

That was the difference, he realized. There weren't tens of millions of nameless faces like it had been in New York City. He was slowly getting to know everyone who worked on the island.

The people who made the resort possible not only worked together, they lived and played together. They were vulnerable and ultimately they were his responsibility.

Alex climbed out of the cart and stood for a minute, undecided. Should he bother Harriet? With her orphans visiting she could be catching up on office work–or even sleeping. He decided to go, but before he could turn around and make his escape the door opened and Harriet stood there smiling at him.

"What a pleasant surprise." She held her hand out to him. "Don't just stand out there. Come inside, Alex. I'm glad to see you."

She *was* glad to see him, Alex realized. Her

clear silver blue eyes held a smile that warmed him. She hadn't changed from her work clothes yet. He knew that because Harriet always slipped into shorts and a tee as soon as she got home and she had answered the door in a simple pale teal silk skirt and matching blouse.

She was also barefoot, a fact that made Alex smile. Harriet always kicked off her shoes as soon she entered the cottage or her office. He knew so many little things about her already, but he wanted to know more–much more. He didn't think he'd ever met a more fascinating creature. It was no wonder he had fallen in love with her.

"You just got in," he said, moving away from the cart. "I was headed to the office and found myself here." He shrugged one shoulder. "I should have called first. Sorry."

Harriet took his hand and drew him inside. "You never have to call first, Alex." Tilting her head she brushed his jaw with her lips. "You are always welcome in my home at any hour, day or night."

"Ah, Harriet." Alex wrapped his arms around her and drew her close. She snuggled against his chest and kissed his neck. They stood that way, just being together, until Harriet broke the silence.

"Would you like some dinner? I was just going

to see what I had in the fridge. I'm famished." She laughed softly. "Must be all the extra outside activity with my girls."

Alex clasped her shoulders and moved her away far enough so he could see her face. "You know what? Let's go out to dinner. Fox and I are scheduled to meet at the circus in a couple hours. We need to finish interviewing the circus folk, but I'd love to have you with me if you can stand it. We could eat there."

Harriet wrinkled her nose. "I've eaten at the amusement park or circus food courts every day this week with the kids. The food is great, but I'm craving a quiet sit down meal and a glass of wine."

"Ah. Of course. I understand." Disappointed, Alex dropped his hands. "In that case I need to get to the office to check some employee records. Maybe I'll see you tomorrow."

Harriet grabbed his hand before he could make his escape.

"Whoa. That doesn't mean we can't have dinner together. We can eat at the employee canteen. And I'd love to go to the circus with you afterwards."

Relief coursed through Alex. He had really wanted to spend time with Harriet even though he had to work. No, he amended, he *needed* to spend time with Harriet. She made everything easier, and if not easier, at least tolerable.

"An excellent plan," he said with a smile. "We'll stop by my office real quick on the way if that's all right with you."

"That works. Let me put on my trainers. The girls keep me on my feet a lot more than I'm used to. Sandals just won't do tonight."

Ten minutes later Alex pulled up in front of the security building. "Would you rather wait here or come in and wait in the lobby? I'll only be a few minutes."

"You go ahead. I'll wait here." Harriet leaned her head back against the seat and closed her eyes. "Don't get distracted. I'm famished."

"I won't."

Alex's office droid Mary snapped to attention behind the half counter as soon as he entered his office lobby. Stocky and muscular with permanent frown lines etched between her eyebrows to make her appear more serious, his droid couldn't be any more different from Harriet's handsome, suave, and debonair Jeeves.

"Sir."

"Good evening, Mary. Anything to report?"

"Yes, sir. The woman whose diamonds went missing called to apologize for the trouble she caused."

"Thank you, Mary. Anything else?"

"No, sir. Just the one call. No visitors."

"Very good." Alex headed for the locked, solid metal doors that led to his office wing. "I'll be in my office for a few minutes, after which I'm heading back to the circus for interviews. If you need me you'll be able to reach me on my link."

"Yes, sir." Mary stepped back against the rear wall and returned to waiting mode.

There was a time, when Alex had first filled the security director position, when the Mary droids had spooked him a little. There were two identical droids, both named Mary, assigned to his office. He alternated them to give them time to perform self-maintenance. No longer spooked by them, he had since come to appreciate their efficiency and uncomplicated ways.

The Mary droids weren't much different from his office, he mused, as he let himself into the windowless space and looked around at the stark decor. No frills, no personality–unless you counted the large, glossy black desk and the expensive communication system that sat on it, or the single bookcase filled with forensic manuals and law books next to the door. There wasn't a single piece of art nor a photo to soften the off-white walls.

He wouldn't mind a holo of Harriet to set on his desk.

The unexpected thought surprised him. Never in his adult life had he wanted a photo or holo of any of the women he'd dated.

The desire to have an image of Harriet to look at while he worked was further proof that she was indeed the one for him. He caught himself smiling and shook his head, glad that no one could see him smiling at nothing. He was a thirty-two year old man–a man with a serious position and responsibility–acting like a lovestruck teenager.

It only took two minutes to call up the list of circus workers and eliminate the ones he and Fox had interviewed earlier. He split the list and sent half to Fox's link and half to his.

A minute later he closed and locked his office behind him and rejoined Harriet in the cart. Three minutes after that they sat under the vine covered pergola adjacent to the employee dining room.

"So." Alex took a sip of the lemon tea he'd ordered. He never drank while working, although he'd insisted on ordering Harriet a white wine even though she'd tried to refuse.

"So." Harriet repeated. She looked at him over her wine glass. "How goes the inquiry into Frank Davis's death?"

Alex looked around to be sure they wouldn't be overheard. He'd chosen a table in the corner and set apart from the other occupied tables so they could not only talk freely, but also enjoy a little intimacy. Thick hedges dotted with large pink flowers surrounded them on two sides. No one lurked on the other side of the hedges.

It wasn't as private as dining on Harriet's lanai, but they weren't surrounded with noisy diners either. Soft blues played on hidden speakers and the quiet conversation from the other outside tables told him that no one was paying attention to their own table.

Alex relaxed and popped a crab-stuffed canapé into his mouth. "I talked to Leonard, Aron, and Roberta at the marina this morning. Aron claims he saw Davis on a bench in front of the hotel speaking with someone from the circus."

"That's why you're interviewing circus workers." Harriet thanked the waitress after she set down their plates and dug into her blackened tuna fiesta salad. "Oh, yum, is this good. Here, have a taste."

Alex took the offered bite. The sushi grade tuna steak had barely kissed a hot grill. The spice rub was perfectly balanced to the sweet tuna and the creamy ranch dressing and crunch of lettuce and raw vegetables set it off.

"Mmmm, that is good. I'll have to order that next time I'm here."

Since they were both hungry they ate in a comfortable silence for several minutes.

"Did any of the circus workers you've talked to so far know Frank Davis?"

Harriet set down her fork and took a sip of her wine, savoring its crisp apple and melon flavors. She observed Alex in the glow of the pergola's tiny lights and the light spilling from the dining room. The candle in the center of their table emphasized his black hair and strong cheekbones, as well as the crook in his nose.

She rubbed absently at her own nose bump and briefly wondered if she would learn the answer to how she sustained the injury once the blocks were removed from her memory, but quickly abandoned the thought when she felt the familiar ache start at the back of her head.

"Are you okay?" Alex's deep blue eyes, eyes that reminded her of the Atlantic ocean on a sunny summer day, filled with concern.

Damn, the man was observant. Too observant sometimes. Harriet smiled. "I'm fine," she assured him. "So, did anyone you talked to know Frank Davis?"

"Yes, as a matter of fact. Eleanor and Simon

Angel took a scuba lesson from Davis. He took them to dive Black Bart's sunken ship."

"I've heard that's a popular dive. I should probably use it in one of my ads for the resort." Harriet made a mental note to learn more about Black Bart and why his ship had sunk in the cove.

"Have you, ah, . . ." Harriet felt her shoulders tighten. Her mouth twisted in an embarrassed half-grimace. "Did you speak with Madame Zaza?"

"Yes. We talked to her this afternoon." Alex watched the tension go out of Harriet's shoulders and reached across the table to cover her hand with his own.

"Don't worry. We won't have to see her tonight. Fox told me about the spooky reading she gave you." Alex squeezed her hand and released it. "She gave us one too."

"What do mean?"

"When Madame Zaza touched Davis's photo she claimed she actually *saw* the murder, but she couldn't see the killer's face. At first she said the killer was a woman, then she changed her mind and said we were looking for a male killer."

"Do you believe her? What if she was trying to steer you away from the real killer?"

Alex considered that for a minute. "Why say anything at all, then?" He shrugged one broad shoulder. "She knew how Davis had been killed even though we haven't made that public. I don't really buy into the telling fortunes act, but I think Madame Zaza probably does possess some psychic ability. I'm keeping an open mind."

By unspoken consent, their conversation moved onto other things.

Harriet told him about her dinner the previous night with Payson and Dr. Bainbridge and her appointment to have her brain mapped. Much to her relief, Alex insisted on accompanying her when she had the procedure done.

They were just finishing their meal when Alex spied a couple being seated.

"Excuse me a moment. I need to have a word with someone." He set his napkin beside his plate and left the table.

Curious, Harriet watched him approach a woman she recognized from the hotel. She watched as Alex placed a hand on the woman's shoulder and spoke to her. She saw tears sheen in the woman's eyes and the woman shook her head, then nodded. Alex squeezed her shoulder and returned to the table.

"What was that about?" Harriet asked as Alex resumed his seat.

"The woman is a hotel maid. This afternoon a hotel guest accused her of theft, only it turned out the husband had locked her diamonds in the hotel's main safe."

"Oh, how awful for the maid."

"Yeah. I just wanted her to know that even though a report had to be put in the hotel files in case something happened in the future with the same guests, no report was made to her personnel files."

Harriet beamed at Alex. "In other words you reminded her that she was considered a valued and trusted employee. You are a lovely, lovely man, Alex Hayes."

Warmth spread through Alex's chest at Harriet's praise even while he felt a bit embarrassed by it.

"You almost finished?" he asked gruffly. "I need to get to the circus and finish those interviews."

Harriet gave him a knowing smile. "Yes, I'm finished. Let's go."

CHAPTER FOURTEEN

When they arrived at the circus gate Alex planted a light kiss on Harriet's mouth as he helped her from the cart. She smiled and kissed him back, lingering for a moment. Here was the man she was meant to love and cherish, she thought, searching his blue eyes for the love she knew she'd find there.

"What?"

Harriet shook her head and smiled. "Nothing. Just thinking about how lucky I am."

The dimple in Alex's right cheek flashed briefly. "Trust me, the feeling is mutual."

The circus was busier than it had been during Alex's earlier visit. Guests were arriving and leaving. Colored lights lit up the night sky. A light breeze carried the scent of hot buttered popcorn.

As they approached the circus gate Harriet watched the slight change in Alex's posture and demeanor and knew that he had mentally moved into full detective mode. Did others see it? Or was she sensitive to his moods because she felt so close to him?

Fox was already waiting for them, along with a burly, dark-haired man he introduced as Tony, Tamara's brother and temporary gate keeper while his sister ate her dinner.

Harriet shook Tony's hand, feeling the strength there. Fortunately he wasn't the type of man who felt the need to impress her by crushing her fingers. She could easily see the resemblance between brother and sister. Tony had Tamara's bright green eyes and the same intelligent look and both were extremely fit.

"Tony says he saw Davis around the resort a few times–in the employee dining room and once here at the circus–but he never spoke with him," Fox explained after the introductions had been made.

"I have a knack for faces," Tony said with a shrug of one well muscled shoulder. "Especially ones I've seen more than once, like Davis. Elle and my cousin Simon spent some time with him scuba diving. You might try them."

"Thanks. We spoke with them earlier today."

Alex replied. “What do you do when you aren’t filling in for your sister?”

“Trapeze. Arial stunts. Tam used to be my partner but she had a bad scare last winter and is taking some time off. I’m working up a few routines with my cousin to fill in until Tam feels ready to fly through the air again.”

A family group with three children approached the gate and Tony excused himself.

“I didn’t know Tamara was a trapeze artist,” Harriet said, as they walked through the gate. “That has to take nerves of steel. I wonder what happened to scare her.” She shuddered. “I can only imagine how frightening it would be to fall.”

Since there was nothing he could say to that, Alex turned to Fox. “I sent you half the list of names we need to interview tonight. I want to split up so we can get through this faster. Write up what you learn and send it to me, then go home and get some sleep. I have a feeling it’s going to be a long day tomorrow.”

“Yes, Boss. See you around, Harry.” Fox gave Alex a mock salute, winked at Harriet, and headed off.

“He’s so charming.”

“Who, Fox?” Alex glanced at the Irishman’s receding back. “It’s the Irish blarney in him. It’s his secret sauce. He has a knack for interviewing people and digging out things they'd rather not talk about."

Harriet suppressed a smile. She agreed with Alex's assessment. Tarbell never ceased to amaze her with what other people readily confided in him. She'd fallen prey to his friendly Irish features and easy charm herself more than once.

"Who do we talk to first?" she asked. Anticipation bubbled through her as she looked around. This was her first visit to the circus after dark. Despite being scaled back for its winter hiatus, the circus looked and sounded much more exciting and exotic than it did awash in bright sunlight.

The colored lights were on and many of the circus people were dressed in full costume even though they would only be performing abbreviated versions of their regular acts.

Harriet knew that the lights, partial acts, and costumes were part of the deal the circus had made with Douglas Wade. They were a small price to pay in return for an expense-free winter home and a place to practice new acts.

The resort guests loved being able to watch an act being developed and see behind the scenes. It made them feel special, connected, a part of the circus in some small way.

Harriet suspected that the Angel Brothers'

take at the gate would increase during the touring season because of word of mouth advertising from the resort guests. Many of the same guests who saw them on the island would not only travel to see the full show when the circus went back on tour, they'd also tell their friends and acquaintances.

A lion roared across the way, reminding her of Hayley and the little girl's obsession with the king of beasts. There was something there, she mused. Maybe the lion made Hayley feel safe and protected. Or it could be that the lion made her feel empowered.

Harriet hadn't pried into the girl's life prior to moving into the orphanage, but she knew that many of the kids had been through horrific experiences. Because of her own life, she knew it was best to let the children share what they were comfortable with. Part of her goal was to give them the tools and confidence to move beyond their bad experiences.

She had made plans to take Hayley and her two friends to the marina the next day and introduce them to water sports in the hopes the girls would want to learn to swim. They loved the water slide, which was encouraging, but the pool at the bottom of the slide was only three feet deep, not deep enough to do much besides float.

One thing she'd learned from the two groups of orphans who had visited the island–with very few exceptions–they were afraid of the water and rarely waded in above their knees.

Harriet wanted to fix that. With three quarters of the planet covered in water, she wanted to give her orphans the ability to save themselves should they ever fall into deep water. And that meant learning to swim, a skill she considered essential for anyone.

There was also the added benefit that the more skills a person possessed, the more confidence they developed.

"What's wrong?"

Harriet started. "What?"

"You were frowning. Is something wrong?"

"Nope. I was just thinking about teaching the orphans to swim." She shook her head and smiled. "It's not important. At least, it's not important right now."

Alex studied her for a moment, then brushed his lips gently across her forehead. "You have a generous and kind heart, Harriet. But then, I already knew that. It's one of the reasons I love you."

Touched by his words, Harriet leaned into Alex. "I love you, too," she said softly. She noticed people watching them and flushed. Never comfortable with public displays of affection, she pulled away and immediately missed his warmth.

"So, who are we seeing first?"

"First up is Giorgio Angel and his trick dogs." Alex brought up a map of the circus on his link, oriented it to where they stood, and pointed to the right, opposite the lions.

"Giorgio and his dogs should be over there." He pocketed the link and twined his fingers with Harriet's, pulling her back to his side. He had no problem with open displays of affection when they involved Harriet.

"We might as well enjoy ourselves while we're here," he whispered into her ear.

Harriet shivered at the feel of Alex's warm breath, making him grin with satisfaction. He abandoned the idea of teasing her further when he spied the stilt walker Lino working with a female partner. Recalling Fox's comment about their ability to see everything going on, he veered toward them.

The female stilt walker wore the same red and white striped pants and white spotted red blouse as Lino, but the similarities ended there. In place of a top hat the woman wore a huge, bright red curly wig. Her shirt strained against a large, obviously fake, bosom that made Harriet wonder how she managed to balance on her tall stilts. Her derriere was equally well padded. Maybe they balanced out.

"Harry!" Lino spotted them and headed their way with his partner in tow. "I'd like you to meet my wife, Salina."

Salina bent down and briefly shook Harriet's hand. Her warm brown eyes sparkled with fun. "I'm very happy to meet you, Harry. Lino told me about seeing you here with three of your little orphans yesterday. We always look forward to seeing them. I hope you'll let me know if there's some way we can contribute or be of use to your program."

"That's very generous of you. I'll add you to my list of volunteers. I'm sure I can find a way for you to help."

Salina's eyes lost their sparkle and grew serious. "All through history orphans have run away from bad situations and ended up working for a circus, you know. We've always taken them in and tried to give them a better life. What you're doing deserves our support. We even have an orphan or two working for Angel Brothers." She smiled and the sparkle returned to her eyes.

"Did you ever see this man hanging around the circus?" Alex passed the photo of Frank Davis up to Salina.

She studied it carefully. "Yes." She handed the

photo back. "He was here . . . maybe a week ago, give or take a day or two. He was walking away from the Big Tent, headed toward the gate."

"What time of day? Early? Late?"

Salina wagged her head, making the wig's massive curls bounce. "Evening. Yes, definitely evening. Right about this time, actually. It was after our evening meal and Lino and I had only been walking maybe a half hour or so. We walk two hours during the day and two at night while we're on the island just to keep our balance up, you know?"

She turned to her husband. "I don't think you saw him, darling. You were busy entertaining those young twin girls who were here with their rather stuffy mother. Remember them?"

"Yes, I remember, and no, you're right, I never saw him."

Alex tucked the photo away in his shirt pocket. "Thanks for your help, both of you. We'll let you get on with your walking."

"Harry, don't forget about finding a way to use us. Maybe we could teach the kids to stilt walk. We can easily make up some short practice sticks." Salina smiled and headed off.

Alex took Harriet's hand again and they headed once more for the dog trainer's tent.

"Well, that confirms Aron's statement that he

saw Davis speaking with someone from the circus. Now if we can just find whoever that was."

They found Giorgio Angel a few minutes later working with his dogs in a small ring set in the center of a medium-sized red and white striped tent. Alex realized there was a theme with the Angel Brothers' colors: blue and white cabanas for food, red and white stripes for the entertainment tents and stilt walkers.

Seven dogs of various sizes and breeds sat in a straight line on one side of the ring, with the three smallest dogs sitting atop boxes. What Alex took to be an obstacle course of some sort with ladders and rings and more boxes had been set up inside the ring.

"Jacques! Vite! Vite! Quickly!" A tall, rangy man with a white goatee stood in the center of the ring and pointed to a small, white terrier. The terrier jumped down from his box and raced up a ladder, through a hoop, down the other side, and returned to his box lickity split.

"Très bien. Très bien. Very good. Good boy, Jacques." Giorgio stepped over to the little terrier and fed him a treat before fondling his ears. The terrier looked up at his master with obvious adoration.

Giorgio stepped to the dog next to Jacques and wagged his finger in the dog's face. "You see how it is done, Hugo?" he asked. "You wish to try again?"

The dog's long pink tongue lolled out of one side of his mouth. He wasn't any breed that Alex recognized. One gray ear stood straight up, the other flopped down. Its sooty gray fur looked wiry and it sported a large moustache and bushy eyebrows. A long, skinny tail swept the tent floor behind it.

"All right, Hugo, Vite! Vite! Quickly now!" Giorgio clapped his hands to encourage the dog.

Hugo stood and yawned, stretched into a downward dog, then padded slowly into the ring. He put one paw on the bottom rung of the ladder, took it off, and sat.

"Ah, mon ami, what am I going to do with you? Perhaps we try a different trick, eh?"

Alex was amused to see Giorgio reward the dog and rub his mismatched ears even though the dog hadn't done anything.

A burst of laughter escaped Harriet's lips. Giorgio turned and smiled at her and shrugged.

"What can I do? These strays show up and I feel compelled to take them in. Eventually I find what they are good at. We should all be so lucky, eh?"

Harriet pulled free from Alex's hand and approached the dogs. She liked Giorgio's philosophy of finding what each dog was good at and building on that aptitude. It should be the same way with people, she mused, as she scratched between the ears of a wide-bodied dog with liver-colored spots and the shortest legs she'd ever seen.

"Are they all strays?" The dog dropped to his belly and rolled onto his back. His short, stubby legs stuck straight up in the air. Harriet laughed at the ludicrous sight but took the hint and rubbed the exposed belly. The dog moaned with happiness.

Giorgio smiled at her. "You are good with them. Yes, they are all strays. Strays are the best, you know–for loyalty and for training. They are grateful for a full belly, for any scrap of love, and for something to do. Every creature likes to feel appreciated and useful. So they work hard once I find their calling." He held out his hand.

"Giorgio Angel, at your service. And you are Miss Harriet Monroe. Word of your orphan program has spread. You are a hero to us circus folk. I myself was once an orphan–before the circus adopted me and gave me a home."

Harriet shook the offered hand and blushed. "Please, call me Harry. The orphan program might have been my idea but it wouldn't happen if it wasn't for all the wonderful people who support it. They're the real heroes, not me."

Alex had lingered near the tent's entrance, content to let Harriet break the ice–something she was very good at, he was learning. He joined them then and reached out a hand as well.

"I'm Alex Hayes, director of security for the resort."

Giorgio shook his hand and immediately returned his attention to Harriet. "In my experience orphans don't get much opportunity to interact with animals–at least not of the friendly four-legged variety. I would be honored if you could find a way for me and my family of canines to help change that."

"I hadn't really considered that aspect of my orphans' lives," Harriet said slowly. "I've tried to discover where the gaps are and begin to address them, but I never considered access to animals. Maybe because I never had any pets of my own growing up."

She beamed at Giorgio. "Thank you for pointing that out. Perhaps I'll stop by tomorrow with the three girls I'm mentoring this week and we can discuss it further. I'm beginning to think the circus has much more to offer my kids than I had realized."

Giorgio nodded and beamed back at Harriet. "Oui. Yes. The circus and orphans are a natural pairing. I shall look forward to seeing you tomorrow. Perhaps the young ladies would like to help me with the training, non? My four-legged friends here would love them, I'm sure."

Giorgio sketched a quick bow and turned his attention to Alex. "Word spread after your visit this afternoon that you are looking for a killer here on the island. What is it that I can do for you, Mr. Hayes? I can assure you that no one in my circus family is capable of murder."

"Everyone is capable of murder, Mr. Angel, if they are pushed hard enough."

CHAPTER FIFTEEN

Once again, Alex pulled Davis's photo from his pocket and showed it to Giorgio. The dogs all watched him with varying expressions. The terrier cocked its head, its dark eyes bright with intelligence. Hugo dropped to his belly, as if he was too tired to sit any longer, and laid his head on his paws.

"That's is the victim, Frank Davis," Alex said, as Giorgio studied the photo. "We have reason to believe that he visited a friend here in the circus. We're trying to locate that friend in the hope that he'll be able to tell us more about Davis. We have very little to go on."

It was the truth, but not all the truth. Alex was afraid if he told the circus people that he suspected one of theirs was connected to the murder, they would close ranks and protect their fellow worker and tell Alex nothing.

He didn't blame them. He'd probably do the same thing, at least until he spoke with the person in question.

So he waited, exhibiting none of the impatience he was feeling, while Giorgio examined the photo.

Giorgio pursed his lips and inspected the photo for a long minute, watched closely by his canine family. Harriet was impressed by how well behaved they were. When Giorgio handed back the photo he was nodding.

"You should try Holden," he said, tapping the picture with his finger. "He partners with Alexander, our senior fire eater. Holden joined us in Belarus, about nine months or so back. I do not know him well as our paths seldom cross so I cannot tell you any more than that."

Giorgio handed the photo back to Alex and lifted one shoulder. "Holden keeps to himself mostly, but I have seen him talking with that man"–he nodded at the photo in Alex's hand–"twice."

"Would this have been in the last week?" Alex asked.

"Once last week, once the week before."

"Did you happen to hear what they were talking about? Were they arguing?"

"No, I didn't hear. No, they didn't appear to be arguing. They seemed . . . pleased." Giorgio shrugged again. "You will have to ask Holden. I only saw them speaking together. That's all I can say with certainty."

Alex thanked him and pocketed the photo. "Where can we find this Holden?"

Giorgio checked his wrist unit and pointed to the Big Tent. "Alexander and Holden are putting on a short performance in a few minutes. Your best bet is to catch them in the main tent when they are done."

"Thank you for your help," Harriet told the dog trainer as they walked out. "I'll see you tomorrow?"

Giorgio bowed deeply. "I shall look forward to meeting your girls tomorrow with the greatest pleasure, Miss Harry."

Harriet left the tent bubbling with enthusiasm over the new possibilities for her kids. Stilt walking, working with animals–both would be skill-building confidence boosters. She wondered if the acrobats would be interested in teaching her kids to tumble.

As they made their way toward the Big Tent,

Alex once again took Harriet's hand. He slanted a sideways look at her.

"Should I be jealous? You seem to have quite an admirer in Giorgio."

While Harriet would never set out to make Alex jealous, it warmed her heart to know that he cared enough about her to feel a little jealousy. She smiled at him and said nothing. Let him wonder.

Alex leaned over to speak into her ear. "You belong to me, sweet Harriet. *Mine*. Never forget that." He gently bit her earlobe, then flicked the bite with his tongue.

Harriet caught her breath and shivered in response. The man knew just how to get to her.

Unfortunately someone called her name before she could think of a suitable reply that would produce the same reaction in Alex.

"Harriet! Fancy seeing you here. Are you going to introduce me to your friend?" Fiona Sprite, dressed in a mini skirt and close-fitting halter top that clearly showed off a well-toned physique, planted herself in front of Alex, giving Harriet no choice but to make the introductions.

"Alex, this is Fiona Sprite, the scriptwriter Cass hired to come up with some ideas for our mystery dinner theater. Fiona, this is the resort's security director, Alex Hayes."

Fiona reached out a hand and Alex automatically took it. When he tried to pull free Fiona held tight. She smiled at Alex coyly, ignoring Harriet entirely.

"My, but you are a handsome devil, aren't you? Big and strong and you *really* have that testosterone thing going on. *Very* sexy. I do appreciate an attractive man. Perhaps we could have dinner sometime while I'm here? Tomorrow night work for you? I hate to waste time. When I see something I want I go after it."

Harriet's mouth dropped open. She couldn't believe her ears. Couldn't Fiona see how close Alex was standing to her? He'd even been holding her hand until Fiona wanted to shake hands with him and he'd had to let go. It had to be obvious to even the blindest of people that she and Alex were a couple.

What was Fiona thinking, asking Alex to have dinner with her?

A furious, jealous heat surged through Harriet and heated her cheeks. This wasn't the first time a woman had made a pass at Alex while she stood beside him. The behavior baffled her. Obviously the man was with someone. Didn't the other women notice? Or did they simply not care, figuring they had the right to make a play for any man who attracted them?

She had to clamp her jaw tight to keep from saying something to Fiona that she might later regret. If she hadn't cared much for Fiona before, she liked her even less after this unpleasant encounter. She forced a tight smile she didn't feel and waited for Alex to handle the pushy scriptwriter.

"I'm flattered, Miss Sprite," Alex said evenly, "but not even remotely interested. I don't think Harriet would appreciate me having dinner with another woman. More importantly, my heart belongs to her. Now if you'll excuse us, we have some business to conduct."

Fiona shrugged one bare, freckled shoulder and gave Alex another warm smile. "Can't blame a woman for trying. Men like you aren't that thick on the ground, you know. If you change your mind you can reach me at the hotel–any time, day or night. See you tomorrow, Harriet." She turned and walked off before Harriet could answer.

"That woman is carrying around a load of aggressive hostility. I'm surprised that Cass hired her." Alex twined his fingers with Harriet's again and set off for the Big Tent.

Harriet looked over her shoulder and watched Fiona head toward the gate. "She told me that she's an orphan. I have the feeling she's still angry about it. I don't think she had an easy time growing up."

"Neither did you and you turned out just fine." Alex leaned over and brushed his lips across her temple.

A warm and fuzzy glow replaced Harriet's spurt of jealousy. She could afford to overlook Fiona's behavior–after all, Alex had declared in public that Harriet had his heart.

She turned her attention once again to enjoying the atmosphere of the circus at night and began to sketch out a new resort ad in her head. She would film the circus after dark and be sure to catch the stilt walkers, Lino and Salina.

Just like with the amusement park, it would be important to capture the sounds of the circus. She could hear the lions, the whinny of a horse, the bright sound of bells ringing at several of the game cabanas, people talking and laughing, the muffled voice of an announcer inside the Big Tent.

They were only halfway across the circus grounds when they heard a scream.

"That sounded like it came from the Big Tent," Harriet said.

Alex dropped her hand and broke into a run. "Get Fox on the link!" he shouted over his shoulder, and disappeared into the groups of people suddenly surging toward the tent.

People pushed past Harriet while she fumbled with her link. She reached Fox and told him there was trouble at the Big Tent, then hurried after Alex.

Fox joined Harriet immediately after she had entered the tent. He grabbed her elbow and guided her through the crowd of onlookers to the center ring where Alex worked over a young man, giving him CPR.

"Get the names of the witnesses," he told Fox between breaths.

Fox began to herd the onlookers to the stand of bleachers on the right side of the tent, took out his link, and began taking names and contact information.

Harriet saw several people sidle back toward the entrance when they realized what Fox was doing. She didn't have the authority to stop them and there was no one else to ask for help.

She stared hard at the departing faces so she would remember them while she pulled out her link again to call Dr. Clarke.

The spa doctor wasn't happy to have her evening meal interrupted but told Harriet she'd be there inside of fifteen minutes. Harriet thanked her and disconnected. Pocketing the link, she pushed through a knot of people who were watching Alex with avid curiosity.

"What can I do?" she asked quietly, kneeling on the opposite side of the man.

"He's not responding. Why isn't he responding?" Alex stopped pumping the man's chest and reached for his link. "I need to contact Dr. Clarke."

"Already done. She's on her way."

"Thanks." Alex checked the man's neck for a pulse one last time and rocked back on his heels. "It's no good. He's dead. He should be alive, but he's dead."

Harriet looked down at the unresponsive man and felt a wave of pity. He looked to be in his mid to late twenties, close to her own age. People her age didn't just drop dead for no reason.

"Do you know what happened?" she asked.

One of the men from a nearby family group overheard and approached them.

"I can tell you. My name is Winston. Elliot Winston. My two sons and wife and I were waiting to see the fire eater. I believe the elder performer"– he pointed to an older man with silver threading his dark hair, standing at the edge of the ring with a shocked expression on his face–"I think he was training this one."

"Did you see what happened?" Alex asked.

The man nodded, swallowed. "Yes."

Harriet watched him steady himself.

"Sorry. I've never watched anyone die before. It was quite . . . dramatic, you know?"

Winston gestured toward the dead man and then put his hand to his throat. "He was about to do that thing where they breathe fire, you know? He swallowed some of that stuff they use, then grabbed his throat and stumbled. At first I thought he had choked, but then he spit out the liquid. He seemed to gasp for breath and he asked the other fire eater for help."

"Did anyone try to help him?" Alex asked, still squatting by the body.

Winston shook his head. "There wasn't time. He collapsed, convulsed for a few seconds, and then was still. He's really dead, isn't he?"

Alex stood, ran a hand through his hair. "Yes, Mr. Winston, he's most definitely dead. If you could give your contact information to my assistant by the bleachers over there, I'd appreciate it. We'll be in touch for a formal statement."

Elliot Winston didn't move. He stared down at the body. "I can't believe it." He looked at Harriet and shook his head.

"Of all the luck." He grinned then. "Wait until I tell them back at the office that I actually witnessed a death at the resort. I'll dine out for a month easy on this story."

Winston turned away and returned to his family. They wandered over to where Fox was gathering names.

Harriet snapped her jaw shut when she realized her mouth was hanging open. She whirled on Alex.

"Did that–that . . . jerk just say what I thought he said? He's happy that he witnessed a death?" Her voice rose on the last word. She took a deep breath and fisted her hands at her sides to stop them from shaking.

"Unbelievable," she muttered. "Just when I'm sure I've seen the worst behavior a person can exhibit, someone shows me that I was wrong."

"Welcome to my world." Any trace of light teasing had left Alex's voice and demeanor. He was all hard cop, and he was pissed. Someone had known they were coming to speak with Holden and had decided to do something about it. It galled him that they had gotten to Holden first.

CHAPTER SIXTEEN

Harriet was still fuming over Elliot Winston's callous attitude toward the young fire eater's death when Dr. Clarke arrived wearing her white spa doctor's coat over a sequined evening dress and carrying her doctor's bag.

"Sorry to take you away from your evening, Eleanor," Alex apologized. "But, as you can see we have a rather sudden unexplained death." He checked his wrist link. "Happened less than fifteen minutes ago."

Dr. Clarke set her black medical bag on the ground beside the body and dropped gracefully to her knees.

"No apologies necessary. I was only having dinner with a friend. How did you get here so fast? And what can you tell me about the deceased?"

"A special friend, I think, given how you're dressed, so I'm doubly sorry to call you away. I hope your friend will wait for you. As for how we got here so fast, Fox and I were already here interviewing the circus people." Alex looked down at the body.

"If my guess is correct, and I'm ninety-nine point nine percent certain that it is, the young man's name is Holden. I believe he was attempting a fire breathing act."

Dr. Clarke looked up quickly. "A fire breather? That shouldn't kill him. They don't actually swallow the flammable liquid. They hold it in their mouths and light the liquid as they spray it out. I saw one once. It's all very dramatic, but a well trained fire eater rarely suffers even a blistered lip. Were there witnesses?"

"Several, in fact. They say Holden spat out something, grabbed his throat, gasped for air, and collapsed. Do you think he had a heart attack? He seems awfully young for heart failure, but he might have had an undetected defect."

Dr. Clarke shook her head and pursed her lips. "That doesn't sound like a heart attack. He would have clutched his chest, not his throat, if his heart had seized. Where is his fire fluid? The stuff he he held in his mouth right before he died?"

"Here."

Harriet recognized the senior fire eater from her wanderings around the circus. His thick, black hair, liberally laced with silver, was brushed straight back from his face, emphasizing prominent cheekbones, a strong jaw, and bright green eyes. His handsome features plus an innate swagger not only made him hard to miss, they marked him as an obvious blood relative of the Angel family.

The elder fire eater had been silently waiting near the side of the ring. When he handed the doctor a glass of clear liquid from the prop table, Harriet could clearly see the shock and sadness in his expression. His hands shook and he used both to hold the glass steady so it wouldn't slosh.

At least the orphan Holden had had one person who cared about him.

"I am Alexander Angel, circus Fire Eater." He took a shaky breath and steadied himself. "I can assure you that we use a very pure lamp oil with few carcinogens. I poured it for Holden myself. This was to be the boy's first act in front of a real audience."

Alexander looked down at the body and swallowed. When he looked up again his eyes filled with tears.

"He was excited. He had studied and practiced hard to learn the skill of working with fire, and even harder on the showmanship." He looked up and caught Harriet's eye. "It isn't all about the fire, you know. It's about engaging the audience and controlling them." A tear made its way down his cheek.

Harriet stepped forward and placed her hand on Alexander's arm. "I'm so sorry for your loss."

Dr. Clarke held the glass a foot from her nose and carefully sniffed the contents before handing it to Alex. "Be careful with that," she told him. "It's lethal if you touch it. Even breathing it can be problematic."

She reached for Alex's free hand and pulled herself to her feet, then looked down at the body and shook her head.

"You'd better check the main supply of lamp oil. Someone added cyanide to the fire eater's fuel." She nodded toward the glass in Alex's hand.

"He never had a chance. Cyanide is a metabolic poison–it prevents the body's cells from utilizing oxygen. He would have died even if you'd been Johnny on the spot."

The elder fire eater made a strangled sound.

"Who would do such a thing? Holden never did anyone any harm. He was a quiet boy who kept to himself."

Harriet found it touching that the older Alexander referred to Holden as a boy even though Holden had obviously been in his twenties. It was obvious to her that there'd been affection between the two men.

She stepped out of the way so Alex could carefully set the glass of fire breathing liquid on the table Holden had used for his props. He frowned at the glass for a moment, then turned to Alexander.

"Mr. Angel, I too am sorry for your loss. Obviously this wasn't an accident. Someone wished you or your apprentice harm. Who would have access to this prop table?"

Alexander lifted one hand in a helpless gesture, let it drop to his side. "Anyone, I suppose. When we are on tour no one outside the circus is allowed inside the Big Tent until showtime and the ring is carefully monitored. But here? Here we have been more lax. There are resort guests wandering around, mingling with the circus folk–you understand?"

"Unfortunately I do. Walk me through the last half hour–make that the last hour. Was the props table in the middle of the ring during that time?"

"No, not the entire time. Bringing the tools of the trade into the ring is part of the act. It sat outside the ring and just inside the rear entrance–that's the entrance we use once the audience is inside. The audience uses the front entrance, we use the rear."

"Okay. So the props table is sitting near the rear entrance. When did you set the glass of flammable liquid on it?"

Alexander's brow furrowed. "I prepped everything a little earlier than usual tonight because Holden was nervous. He checked everything twice and then we walked around for a bit outside to help him relax."

Alex frowned and shook his head. "So the bottom line is that anyone could have accessed the props table. They could have entered the tent by the main entrance, wandered over to the table, discreetly dropped the cyanide into the glass, then popped out the rear entrance. All in under a minute."

Harriet could see that the questioning had helped Alexander. His tears had dried and his eyes were bright with anger. He jabbed a finger at Alex.

"You will find who did this. You will find who stole the future of that innocent young man."

"Yes," Alex answered grimly, "I promise you I will find the person who killed your apprentice."

Harriet stepped aside to make room for the gurney and two attendants. She realized that the doctor must have called the attendants right after she'd spoken with her. Dr. Clarke had them don masks, gloves, and coveralls before she let them bag Holden's body and remove it.

The sight reminded her that Alex had been giving the dead man CPR.

"Dr. Clarke?"

"Yes?" The doctor never took her eyes off the attendants as they moved the body.

"Ah, Alex was giving the deceased CPR. Do you think–is it possible that he picked up some of the cyanide?"

Dr. Clarke's head whipped around.

"Alex!"

Alex interrupted his conversation with Alexander. "You have something already?"

"No. You were giving the deceased CPR? Did you give him mouth to mouth resuscitation?"

Alex shook his head. "There wasn't time. He died before I could start."

The tension went out of the doctor's shoulders and face. "You're damned lucky. If you had given the kiss of life it would have been the kiss of death for you.

"I'll have the body sent to the lab on the mainland and autopsy it tomorrow, unless you need results sooner," Dr. Clarke told Alex. "But I can tell you that I'm reasonably positive cyanide killed your young man." She closed her doctor's bag with a resounding snap.

"You know how to reach me if you need me again. Good night, Harriet."

Harriet watched Dr. Clarke stride to the tent's entrance and disappear. She had the feeling Dr. Clarke didn't particularly care for her, but she suspected she wasn't being fair. The only time she had interacted with Dr. Clarke was over dead bodies. No one would feel too friendly under those circumstances.

She breathed a little easier once the attendants had taken away Holden. Even though she had seen several dead bodies since taking the job on the resort, the sight of them still hit her hard. She wondered if a person ever got used to it.

Alex must have seen hundreds of dead bodies during his career. Had he become jaded to the sight of the deceased while working as a NYC murder cop?

She hoped not. What a terrible thing that would be. To become immune to the sight of the dead would be a sign that you were losing your connection to your fellow man. Losing your humanity.

She looked at Alex and knew in her heart that

that hadn't happened to him. He was a man who cared deeply. Maybe too deeply. It was far more likely that he'd left his NYC job because dealing with senseless death became too much to bear.

"Harriet."

"What?" Startled, Harriet realized Alex had been speaking to her. "I'm sorry. I was thinking about something."

"Care to share?"

"Maybe later. What can I do to help?"

Alex looked toward Fox. There were still a good dozen people left to speak with. "You don't have to hang around. I'll probably be several more hours at least. Could be even longer. I need to speak to all the circus people again while the evening is fresh in their memories and get their whereabouts for the hour before Holden's act."

Harriet tried not to show her disappointment. "Are you sure? I don't mind hanging around."

"Go home. If I'm not too late I'll come to the cottage. Otherwise I'll just grab a few hours shut eye in my apartment." He gave her a rueful smile. "I was having a nice time. We'll have to do this again, soon."

"Only next time let's skip the dead body." Harriet turned and walked out of the tent.

CHAPTER SEVENTEEN

Harriet gathered her three lively charges the following morning and headed for the resort's marina.

She loved the marina. While not a working waterfront, it gave her the flavor of one with its gray, weathered docks and variety of boats. It smelled of briny seaweed and varnish and fresh salt air and it sounded right, with gulls calling overhead and waves slapping gently against boat hulls and the undersides of the docks.

She felt a brief pang of homesickness for the Portland waterfront that she had once roamed with Solly when they were homeless street urchins. She certainly didn't miss those homeless days, fraught with challenges no young teen should have to face, but she missed the magic of the waterfront itself, a waterfront at the opposite end of the spectrum from where she lived now.

Florescent orange sails bobbed and skittered across the water close to shore–a group of teens learning to sail on the resort's small, easily handled Sunfish. Harriet watched them for a few minutes, grinning when one daring young man tried to show off and dumped himself into the water.

Unlike the cold waters of the North Atlantic, the ocean surrounding the resort island was a comfortable temperature. Undaunted by his spill, the boy laughed, pulled himself onto the shallow hull of the Sunfish, and took off again.

"Can we do that, Mizz Mun-row?" Hayley eagerly climbed out of the cart and pointed at the Sunfish. "That looks like fun."

"It sure does," Harriet answered. "To be honest I've never tried it myself although I've always wanted to."

"Why haven't you tried it?" Amber Lee asked, coming to stand beside Hayley. "Is it too expensive?"

The tone of the young girl's voice sounded so matter-of-fact that Harriet knew "too expensive" was a phrase Amber Lee heard often.

"As a matter of fact, once a guest pays to stay

on the island everything is included, so no, it isn't too expensive. I just haven't had the time."

"So does that mean we're going to try it?" Dorian, the third member of Hayley's trio, came around the cart and joined them. Her blue eyes looked worried.

"No one has to do anything they don't want to do," Harriet assured her. "I thought we would start with a short ride in a glass-bottom boat and look at all the creatures who live underwater."

Harriet had spent her time waiting for Alex the previous night planning ways to get the girls interested in doing things that involved the ocean. Alex still hadn't shown up by the time she fell asleep, but she had come up with a few ideas for the girls.

Leonard came to the door of the marina office and greeted her with a wave and a smile. "Who are these lovely ladies?" he asked, bending down to shake each one's hand.

The girls introduced themselves while Harriet looked on with pride. Her orphans generally arrived at the resort displaying one of two attitudes. They were either brash and loud in an effort to cover up their insecurity and attract attention, or they were extremely shy and withdrawn because they were afraid of setting a foot wrong and possibly being punished.

Either way, all of the orphans who had visited the island to that point had been insecure–and who could blame them? The world had let the orphans down. They didn't know who they could count on, and they didn't have enough life experience to count on themselves.

During one of her conversations with an orphanage matron, the matron had complained to Harriet about the children always bouncing off the walls. Harriet was fairly certain that one of the reasons for their insecurity was that the orphans' lives were over-restricted and over-regulated.

Knowing that a person could only gain confidence by experimenting and doing, Harriet decided to address the orphans' insecurities by giving the girls opportunities to try everything and anything that interested them.

She also encouraged them to be children–to have fun, in other words–something their lives sorely lacked. She encouraged them to run and shout on the beach until they drooped with exhaustion. She let them race from ride to ride in the amusement park, encouraging their enthusiasm. She let them choose what they wanted to eat, although she did insist upon healthy food before dessert. And she tried to teach them whatever skills presented themselves.

So far her plan seemed to be working. She could see the changes in the way the children carried themselves, and how they approached new things with an eagerness they had lacked when they first arrived on the island.

Hayley, Amber Lee, and Dorian had all fallen into the the second, painfully shy group. It had taken two days for them to understand that they wouldn't be punished for acting their age. Since that shift they'd been irrepressible. Harriet smiled with pleasure every time she thought about the positive changes they'd made.

"I've had the boat prepped," Leonard told Harriet. "Baby Rose is home with Dorinda so I thought I'd take you out myself. I could use a little recreation. If you don't mind, that is," he added hastily.

"We'd love to have you give us a tour of the reef, wouldn't we, girls?"

Leonard beamed at the chorus of yeahs. He put a Back Soon sign in the door and locked the marina office, then led the way to the docks, patiently answering a continuous stream of questions from the girls.

Harriet brought up the rear, content to observe. Rides over the reef in one of the glass-bottomed boats was a must-do for the orphans. She made sure everyone got scheduled for a ride during their week stay.

She considered the rides to be not only entertaining, but also educational. Like flying in a shuttle from the mainland and exploring parts of the island, the view of life under the ocean's surface was yet another way to broaden the orphans' limited view of the world.

The girls exclaimed over the large red starfish that crawled across the mussel beds beneath the docks, their fat arms moving with slow precision as they hunted their prey. At Harriet's suggestion, the girls lay on their stomachs and touched the seaweed anchored to the dock pilings, giggling over how slimy it felt.

Leonard fastened the girls into life jackets and helped them board the boat, then handed a jacket to a grinning Harriet.

"What?"

Harriet shook her head. "Nothing really. I was just thinking about how much fun this is. I love visiting the reef, especially with the kids."

"I know what you mean," Leonard said with a grin. "Why do you think I volunteered to take you out?"

It didn't take long to reach the reef that sat just off the island's western shore. Leonard and

Harriet patiently identified everything they could put a name to. The girls were thrilled when an octopus left his hidey hole and gave them a show, changing colors as he crossed living coral and rocks and sand.

"I wish I could do that," Dorian said wistfully."It's like his super power. I'd make sure Mrs. Barlow never found me."

Harriet smiled at Dorian. "It would be a neat trick, wouldn't it? It's even better than a cloak of invisibility because you never leave it behind. Who is Mrs. Barlow?"

"She's our teacher," Amber Lee answered. All three girls were lying on their stomachs on the bottom of the boat so Harriet couldn't see their faces. She'd learned a lot from listening to them all week however, and she knew from the disgust in Amber Lee's voice that Mrs. Barlow was not well liked.

"Is she a strict teacher?" She probed gently, not wanting to upset them but sensing that Mrs. Barlow had been singled out for a reason.

"Worse," Hayley said. "I don't think she likes little girls. We get punished a lot more than the older kids. She's always making us clean the bathrooms and scrub the hallways because"–she pitched her voice in what Harriet assumed was an imitation of the teacher–"We need to learn what our lives will be like when we grow up."

Harriet stilled. She felt a cold fury wash over her. She caught Leonard's eye and grim expression so she knew he'd had the same reaction. All bullies sucked, but an adult bullying a powerless child was the worst kind of bully.

"She especially doesn't like little girls with red hair," Dorian said glumly. "She says my red hair is a sign that I have the devil in me so she has to punish me extra to get him out." She turned her head and looked at Harriet. Tears pooled in her large blue eyes.

"I don't want the devil in me, Miss Monroe."

Harriet didn't hesitate. She plucked Dorian off the bottom of the boat and set the little girl on her lap. Wrapping her in her arms, she pulled Dorian close and rested her cheek on the girl's fiery red hair.

"You listen to me, Dorian. You do *not* have the devil in you. Mrs. Barlow is gravely mistaken. Your hair is ab-so-lute-ly beautiful. Why, I know grown women who want hair your color so badly that they have their own hair dyed red. And you know what?"

"What?"

"Their dyed hair never looks as pretty as

yours. You know what I think? I think Mrs. Barlow is jealous of your beautiful hair."

"Really?" The hope in Dorian's voice made Harriet's throat constrict. She tightened her arms, willing Dorian to absorb the liking and affection she felt for the girl.

"I would never lie to you, Dorian. You know that, right?" Harriet felt Dorian's head nod beneath her cheek. "All right then. Listen carefully. Your red hair is a gift. Not everyone can wear red hair and look beautiful in it the way you do, you know. One day you will grow up to be a striking, beautiful woman."

Gradually the tension eased from Dorian's little body. She made no effort to rejoin her friends in the bottom of the boat. She seemed content to sit on Harriet's lap and be cuddled.

It occurred to Harriet that the orphans probably received very little human contact of a cuddling nature. It was no wonder they liked to hold her hand and be hugged. It also explained why they pressed close to her whenever they could. They were only seeking what every human sought–the warmth of safe human contact.

Harriet made a silent vow to get Mrs. Barlow fired and make sure the teacher never found another position working with children. And she knew just the man who could see to it.

She made a mental note to call Payson later and ask him to contact the resort owner. As the richest man on the planet, Douglas Wade held a lot of clout, especially with orphanages who were eager for his patronage.

"What's that?" Amber Lee pointed at an object beneath them.

"That's an old anchor," Leonard steered the boat in a slow circle so the girls could get a good look at the object.

"That anchor probably broke free from a ship during a storm and was lost. It looks pretty old. See the barnacles growing all over it? This island was once a popular spot for pirates, you know. They used it to hide out and get fresh water for their ships."

"They buried their treasure here too," Hayley said. "I found a treasure map yesterday. Want to see?" She reached behind her and fumbled with the zipper on her fanny pack. When she got it open she pulled out the map she'd found the previous day.

"It's only half a map," she explained, handing it to Leonard. "I think a pirate must have lost it."

Leonard took the map and inspected it. "It certainly looks like a real map," he said. "What makes you think it's a map of this island?"

"Because I found it here," Hayley told him.

She crawled over to Leonard, leaned on his lap, and pointed at the map. "I don't know what part of the island it shows though. Can you tell?"

"Well, let me see." Leonard put his arm around Hayley and tucked her against his side so they could look at the map together.

"See these indents here?" He traced a section of the map with his finger. "I think these are the coves on the west side of the island. This is Blackbeard's Cove, and here's Black Bart's Cove with the partially sunken pirate ship, and Morgan's Cove. Kidd's cove and the marina cove aren't here, though."

"That's because it must be on the other half of the map!" Hayley said, delighted.

Leonard pointed again. "Here's the mangrove swamp on the southern tip of the island. And here are one and a half of the three mountains and this looks like the lagoon that's now at the top of the waterslide. It's a good map."

Hayley beamed up at him. "So I was right. It *is* a map of this island."

"Too bad this half of the map doesn't have an X to show where the treasure is buried," Leonard said, handing the map back to Hayley. He gave her a hug. "But it's still a really, *really* cool find."

Harriet was glad to see that Hayley didn't

seem the least bit bothered by the fact that her map didn't lead to a buried treasure.

Hayley laid back down next to Amber Lee and rolled onto her back. She held the map above her and studied it.

"There's an X," she said in a puzzled voice. She sat up and set the map in her lap.

"But I can't see it when I put the map on my lap. Amber Lee, look." Hayley lay back down and held the map above her again so the sun's rays shone through it. Amber Lee rolled over and inspected the map.

"I see the X! Hayley, it's the X for the treasure!"

"Mizz Mun-row, look!" Hayley handed the map to Harriet. "Hold it up to the sun," she instructed.

Harriet held up the map. Sure enough, there was a very faint X near the lagoon, but it was so faint it was impossible to tell if the mark had been made deliberately or if it was simply a random mark. She wasn't about to crush Hayley's enthusiasm, however.

"Looks like an X to me." She handed the map back to Hayley who carefully zipped it back into her fanny pack.

"I'm hungry," Hayley announced. "Amber Lee, aren't you hungry?"

Amber Lee shrugged one shoulder. "Not really. Ow." She rubbed her arm and glared at Hayley.

"Dorian, are you hungry?" Harriet asked. "We've been out here for a while. We should probably get out of the sun before you get a sunburn. That's the only drawback about being a redhead–you have to watch that you don't burn."

She noted the look of satisfaction on Hayley's face and figured Hayley must really be hungry. The girl seemed to have a bottomless pit for a stomach and could really pack the food away. Fine by her. Let the kids eat anything and as much as they wanted. There was no bad food served on the island. Even the desserts were low in fat and sugar.

It was unlikely that Hayley ever had the chance to eat her fill at the orphanage, Harriet mused. Limited budgets meant that food was most likely rationed. She made another mental note, this one to look into restaurant food waste and the possibility of channeling it somehow to nearby orphanages.

Leonard caught Harriet's eye. "So, are we ready to head back?" When she nodded he steered the boat toward the marina. Before long the girls were tossing the boat bumpers over the side and jumping onto the dock to help Leonard tie the boat up.

Harriet gave a hand where needed and praised the girls for their help. After walking Leonard back to his office where the girls gave him an enthusiastic thank you, she herded them into a cart.

"Okay, where do you want to eat?" she asked Hayley.

"I thought I'd get room service."

Harriet barely concealed her surprise. Room service was not among the options she had expected to hear.

"Really? Why do you want to eat in your room? We can go anywhere."

"I want to write about the reef in the journal you gave me."

"All right." There was no way Harriet was going to even attempt to talk Hayley out of her decision. Their week was all about learning that they had choices in life and the freedom to make them without anyone contradicting or denying them.

Secretly she was pleased that Hayley was embracing her journal. Providing each girl with a pretty hardcover blank book embossed with their names and a set of colored pencils and a pen had been one of her hit or miss ideas.

When she presented each girl with their blank journal, Harriet told them it was a place to write down their experiences and thoughts, a place to draw whatever they liked, a place to begin tracking their life going forward.

She knew that the girls' lives would change because of their time on the island. The girls themselves would change. She hoped that in the future some of them would look back in their journals and see not only how those changes had come about, but also the different ways they had changed.

She wished that she had had the extra money to buy a journal after she had run away from her aunt's house. Looking back had a way of making clear how far one had moved forward in life. There were times she still felt like that fifteen year old, muddling through, naive to the ways of the world. During those moments she could use a reminder of how much she had grown.

"We're *all* going to write in our journals," Hayley announced as Harriet pulled into the hotel parking lot. She smiled at the girls as they climbed out of the cart.

"That's terrific. Do you want to do something later? We can go to the amusement park if you want."

"I'm not sure. Thanks, for the boat ride, Mizz Mun-row. See ya." Hayley grabbed Amber Lee's and Dorian's hands and led them toward the hotel.

Bemused, Harriet watched the girls disappear into the lobby. Normally she would have walked them to their room but Hayley had been in too great a hurry.

It didn't occur to her to question why Hayley was in a hurry until later.

CHAPTER EIGHTEEN

Alex lifted his boots onto his office desk, leaned his head back, and closed his eyes. Lord, he was tired.

It had taken until four in the morning to interview every last person at the circus. He'd sent Fox home, taking the last few interviews himself, and told him to report in at nine instead of eight, then had driven straight to his office when he finished talking to the last person.

He had wanted nothing more than to drive down to Mermaid Cottage and crawl into bed with Harriet, but it wouldn't have been fair to wake her up when she still had a few hours left to her night. So he had continued to work through the night instead and now he was paying for it.

His eyes felt dry and gritty and he had a

headache and a sour stomach from all the coffee he'd consumed. His sparsely decorated office felt more stark than usual. He'd finally turned off the overhead lights because they glared off his empty white walls and shiny black desk and made his vision jump.

He smelled of sour sweat and badly needed a shower and a fresh shirt. A shave wouldn't hurt either, he thought ruefully, rubbing his hand over his face.

His office didn't even have a window he could open to let in the ocean breeze and clear the fog from his brain. For the first time since taking the job as security director for the resort, he resented his impenetrable cave of an office.

He pictured Harriet asleep in her lovely big bed with its gauzy white bed curtains and gentle breeze blowing in through the bedroom's lanai doors. If they were married he could have gone home to her no matter the hour.

He was beginning to think that he had been too hasty when he decided he wouldn't ask Harriet to marry him until her memories were restored. He couldn't even remember now what his reasoning had been. Some bullshit that it would be better for her if they waited.

It was probably closer to the truth to say that he'd been afraid that once she regained all her memories she would change–and maybe she wouldn't love him anymore.

Coward. He had finally found a woman he loved with every fiber of his being. One who loved him back. What was he waiting for?

There were always going to be nights like this one. He would always be dealing with murder, he could see that now. Murder was a thread that ran through his life, beginning with his sister's murder.

For some reason he had been chosen to stand for the dead.

Despite his hope that working for the Island Resort would take him away from death and killing, it turned out that murder happened everywhere, even on a lovely tropical island where people were supposed to be relaxed and happy. He might as well accept that this was his lot in life and make the best of it.

He rubbed his tired eyes with a thumb and forefinger and shook his head. There would always be nights when he couldn't make it home until the small hours.

Home.

What a sweet word. Until Harriet, no place had felt like home since he'd lost his sister Allysa. Knowing that Harriet waited for him no matter the hour would make the long work nights tolerable.

It could take years for doctors to fix the damage that had been done to her brain. And wouldn't it be easier for Harriet to deal with the process knowing she had him at her side, just like it would help him to have her at his side?

They'd only known each other a few months, but when everything clicked, when everything felt right, what did that matter? It was foolish for him to wait any longer. He loved her. He needed her.

He imagined crawling into bed and holding her warm supple body. She always smelled good–an honest, clean smell of citrusy shampoo and soap and the essence he identified as uniquely Harriet.

The comm unit on his desk beeped, interrupting his thoughts. Time to focus on work again.

Alex sighed and opened his eyes. The reports he had requested on the male Angel Circus members had come in. He took his feet off the desk with a groan. The old adage that there was no rest for the wicked had it all wrong. It was more accurate to say that there was no rest for the weary who chased the wicked.

Grabbing the keyboard, he began to sift through the reports.

He found nothing that alarmed him and a few things he had expected. Old drug charges with suspended sentences or warnings, a couple of assault charges on Simon Angel that were eventually dropped. He took a closer look at those.

Apparently the trick horse rider had a jealous streak and a few unwise men had dared to hit on his bride.

He couldn't blame Simon for defending what he considered his. Eleanor Angel was incredibly beautiful and probably attracted more male attention than her husband liked. None of the assaults had been particularly serious.

Simon wasn't his man. He was fully engaged with his wife and their act.

Giorgio the dog man had told Harriet the truth. He had been orphaned at fifteen and joined the circus not long after in Versailles, France. That explained his mix of French and English. He was what he appeared to be–a man who loved animals and found ways to get the best from them.

Giorgio had been right about Holden–the fire eater's murdered apprentice had also been an orphan. Like many, he had left the orphanage as soon as he'd turned sixteen, after which he had wandered the U.S., skipping from one low paying job to another, never landing anywhere for more than a month or two until hooking up with Angel Brothers.

He had a minor record, a few misdemeanors for shoplifting.

Holden had joined the circus when they did a brief tour of the States only six months before. Alex had seen many youngsters like Holden in NYC, tossed from what passed as group homes because the law said they were legally adults at sixteen, even though most of them needed a few more years of seasoning before they were truly ready to look after themselves.

Mostly they either prostituted themselves or they dealt drugs at the lowest level of the supply chain–or they did what Holden did and took the lowest paying jobs. If Angel Brothers hadn't come along when they did Holden's misdemeanors would have eventually escalated to real crimes–and jail time.

Holden had been lucky to find a home with the circus–until someone had decided he needed to die.

Alex flipped to the next report. There was very little on Sugo the lion tamer. The fact that he had once been married to Madame Zaza made Alex's eyebrows go up. Alex hadn't requested background reports on any of the women working the circus, but Sugo's report mentioned that Madame Zaza was also an orphan.

He sat back a minute and stared at the screen. Madame Zaza managed the Angel Brothers circus. How did someone not born into the family end up with the top position in the family business? He made a mental note to dig deeper into Madame Zaza and Sugo.

Alex steepled his fingers and tapped his forefingers against his chin while he thought. Madame Zaza had given him an unasked for vision, or reading. He really didn't know what to call it. She had told them a woman murdered Frank Davis, then changed her mind and claimed that it was a man.

Had he been foolish to limit his suspect list to men? Some of the circus women were strong. They could have hit Davis with a rock and stuffed him into the water slide, especially if they'd been standing near the top of the slide at the time.

He shook his head and sighed. No. He was looking for a man. He felt it in his gut. Until he found evidence that said otherwise he would follow his instincts.

Aron from the marina had seen Davis speaking with a man wearing the circus employee red tee shirt. Harriet had overheard a conversation between two men that could be linked to

Davis's murder. Harriet had assumed that it had been a conversation between two adult men, not a man and a woman.

Holden had been large. At least six foot, broad shouldered and fit–like everyone else connected to the circus. They worked hard and had the muscles to show for it. Holden could have easily killed Davis.

If Harriet's overheard conversation connected to Davis's murder–and he felt strongly that it did–then there had been three people involved in some scheme involving a hidden treasure on the island. One of those three–Davis–was now dead.

Holden's death made a certain sense if he was the second man. Perhaps this was a classic example of a falling out among thieves. If so, killing the fire eater could be considered short-sighted. Wouldn't it take one person much longer to search for a treasure than it would two men, or three?

It didn't make any sense.

His brain and body were too tired. He was beginning to think in circles. He needed to take a step back, get a fresh perspective.

He sifted through the remainder of the reports and made a few notes, then checked his wrist unit. Harriet would just be getting ready for a run on the beach before she got ready for work.

A run on the beach would be just the thing to clear his head and order his thoughts. He shut down his comm unit and ran up to his apartment, grabbed a pair of shorts and a tee shirt and a fresh change of work clothes and jumped on his Triumph. He didn't have the patience to take one of the resort's slower, quieter carts.

The Tiger roared to life, a sound that always gladdened Alex's heart and quickened his blood. He smiled in anticipation of Harriet's warm welcome, knowing that she would hear him coming well before he arrived at her cottage and she would be waiting for him at the door.

CHAPTER NINETEEN

Harriet was on her lanai, doing her pre-run stretches and waiting for Solly to join her when she heard Alex's motorcycle coming toward the cottage. She frowned, suddenly worried. Alex only used his Tiger when he needed to get away from the resort or to get somewhere in a hurry.

Solly walked out of his cottage with his trainers in his hand. She couldn't help but notice that he looked even better than he had before almost dying. And happier than she'd seen him in . . . maybe ever.

She really needed to meet Solly's new friend Chef William. Any man who could put a glow on her best friend was someone she wanted to know.

"Harry?" Solly looked over at her, his eyebrows bunched in a frown. "That sounds like Alex. Is something wrong? Did he call?"

"I don't know what's wrong. The last time we spoke he was getting set to interview people after that fire eater's murder." Harriet jumped off the lanai into the soft sand.

"I'll go see what's up. Be right back." She walked around the cottage to the front just as Alex swept into Mermaid's narrow parking pad.

"Good. You haven't left yet.'" he said.

Alex's voice sounded hoarse and raspy and he looked like hell. Harriet could see the lines and shadows of weariness around his eyes and mouth as soon as he removed his shades. His eyes were bloodshot and he still wore yesterday's rumpled clothes.

Knowing Alex, he hadn't stopped for food or rest since she had left him at the circus.

"I was hoping to run with you this morning. I need a change of scenery. Do you and Solly mind?"

Harriet stepped up to him and wrapped her arms around him. "You're always welcome," she said softly.

Alex hugged her tight and dropped his face into her hair. He needed this. He needed her.

Some of the tension began to seep from his body. "I need to change. Give me a minute?"

"We'll wait on the beach for you." She gave him a squeeze and headed back between the cottages. Solly had his trainers on and was stretching when she rejoined him.

"Alex is coming with us. I told him we'd wait on the beach."

"Is he okay?"

Harriet gave a brief head shake and headed toward the water. Solly joined her.

"He's never okay when it comes to murder," she said quietly. "He takes it personally I think, and he feels that he has to give it everything he has, to–" She lifted a hand, searching for the right words.

"I don't know. To make it as right as he can, I guess. He tries to balance the scales of justice, even though no amount of balancing can bring back the dead." She filled Solly in on the apprentice fire eater's murder.

Solly gave Harriet's arm a sympathetic squeeze. "Finding justice is a big job, but if anyone can do it I'd put my money on Alex."

"Thanks for waiting. I needed some fresh air." Dressed in loose shorts and a tee that stretched across his well muscled chest, Alex joined them.

"Glad to have you, Alex. You're always welcome to run with us. I might even get a little more speed out of Harry with you around." Solly gave a quick yank on Harriet's ponytail and grinned.

"Jerk." Harriet took off at a slow, warm up speed with Solly on one side and Alex on the other. Being sandwiched between two beautiful men who also happened to be the two people she loved most in the world wasn't a bad way to start the day, she mused.

No one wasted their breath talking. It was a time to breathe in the salty air and the scent of stranded seaweed drying above the tide line, and to listen to the gentle waves sizzling along the beach.

Because they ran together nearly every day, she was used to matching steps with Solly. Alex quickly picked up their rhythm and it wasn't long before she felt they were running as a single unit. A soft but steady morning breeze blew in their faces and cooled their sweat before it had a chance to soak their shirts.

The steady rhythm of their matched steps thudding in the packed sand grew hypnotic, pushing all thought from Harriet's brain.

Gradually they increased their speed until she was running full out. Alex pulled ahead and Harriet let him go, sensing that he needed to flush his system of all the ugliness from the previous night. Since his near brush with death, Solly no longer pushed faster than her own pace and they continued to run in tandem.

When they reached the mangrove swamp Alex was there waiting for them, walking in circles to keep the lactic acid from building up in his muscles. They turned again as a unit and headed back toward the cottages at a much slower jog.

"Do you want to talk about it?" Solly asked, once their breathing had slowed enough to make speech possible again.

Alex took so long to answer Harriet figured he was going to ignore Solly's question.

"I have two murders," Alex began slowly. "You already know about Frank Davis. Because of a conversation Harriet overheard while at the circus I'm linking Davis with two other people on the island, one of whom I believe is with the circus."

"Are you sure about that?" Solly asked. "It seems to me that the two people Harry heard talking could just as easily have chosen to meet at the circus. That doesn't mean they were necessarily part of the circus."

"I spoke with someone who saw Davis meeting with a male circus employee in front of the hotel. While he did have some innocent, work related doings with a few of the circus folk, that meeting feels significant to me."

"Why?"

Harriet kept silent and let Solly ask questions. He and Alex had become good friends after Solly had helped Alex solve another murder and she knew that Alex respected Solly's thought processes.

"Because . . . " Alex gave Solly's question serious consideration. "Because if the meeting had been work related, it would have taken place either at the marina or at the circus," Alex answered slowly. "The fact that it took place at the hotel feels significant. They didn't want to be seen together where the meeting would be noticed by co-workers."

He shrugged. "It's no more than a gut feeling but it feels *right*."

They all slowed to a walk to finish their cool down. The sun had climbed above the trees to the east, bleaching the sky to a pale blue. A flock of white terns began to cry and dip into the water, attacking a school of small bait fish.

"Okay, I'll buy the gut feeling," Solly said. "So, we have three people looking for treasure on the island. One is dead, and according to the conversation Harry overheard, he was most likely killed by one of his partners. We have an unknown male with the circus, who may or may not be dead, depending on if that second male is the fire eater. What was his name?" Solly looked at Harriet.

"Holden."

"Right, Holden. So, either two of the three partners are now dead or Holden was killed for another, unrelated reason."

"That's my thinking." Alex wiped his face on the sleeve of his tee shirt and grimaced when he caught a whiff of himself. He desperately needed a shower. Out of the corner of his eye, he caught Harriet grinning and knew she'd seen him. He gave her a rueful smile.

"You can shower at my place," she assured him.

The thought of taking a shower with Harriet cheered Alex immensely. He grinned at her and winked.

"I think we go on the assumption that Holden is the second treasure hunter," Solly continued a little louder, and lightly punched Harriet's arm.

"Stop flirting. We're trying to conduct serious detective work here."

Harriet knew by the humorous glint in Solly's eye that he wasn't really put out. She stuck her tongue out at him but immediately sobered.

"Two dead men *is* serious," she agreed. "I agree with you that Holden was one of the three treasure hunters. What I can't figure out is how he connected with Davis. They're from two different worlds. But it's a stretch to think that there's a fourth person involved in this."

"The question is, why kill Holden now?" Alex asked, his mind back on murder. "It makes no sense. Wasn't one of the people you overheard speaking upset because searching for the treasure would be easier with three people than two?"

"Yes." Harriet thought back to the conversation behind the circus cabana. "My guess is that I most likely heard Holden telling Davis's killer that he shouldn't have killed Davis."

"Okay. But why kill Holden?"

"I can think of two reasons the killer decided to eliminate Holden," Solly said.

Both Harriet and Alex turned their heads to look at him.

"One, he thought Holden was losing his grip and was no longer trustworthy, so the killer eliminated him before he talked."

"And two?" Alex asked.

"The killer found Davis's half of the map and doesn't need help searching because he knows where the treasure's buried."

"The map!" Harriet stopped walking. "Alex, I forgot to tell you. One of my girls found half a map tucked under a rock by the water slide steps the day before yesterday. The map looks like it might be old, but someone had laminated it to protect it. Other than some dirt stains it was in pretty good condition, considering. Hayley is convinced that it's a pirate's treasure map."

"And you're just telling me this now?"

Alex didn't sound or look happy.

"Sorry." Harriet winced. "I meant to mention it to you, but then I forgot about it. I thought the map was most likely a fake left there to fool someone.

"Leonard and I took Hayley and her two friends out on the glass bottom boat to look at the reef yesterday and Hayley showed Leonard her map. She carries it in her fanny pack in case she sees the pirate so she can return it to him. She's really sweet that way."

Harriet saw the glower on Alex's face and knew he wasn't interested in her opinion of Hayley's disposition. She swallowed and hurried on.

"Leonard identified the mangrove swamp and the lagoon that feeds into the waterslide on the map. Then Hayley was lying in the bottom of the boat and she held it up to the sun and found an X. You know, as in, X marks the treasure spot."

"Could you see an X?" Solly asked, curious.

Harriet hesitated. "I saw a mark that could be an X. It was very faint, but . . . yes, I'd have to say there was an X on the map–but you'd expect there to be, wouldn't you? If someone was trying to fool a kid, I mean."

"I want you to take me to Hayley as soon as we get cleaned up." Alex grabbed her hand and and began to pull her toward the cottage.

"All right, but don't be surprised if she won't give you the map," Harriet grumbled. "She's pretty invested in the story she's built around it."

The hair on the back of Harriet's neck stirred when Alex turned to look at her. His dark blue eyes looked as cold as the north Atlantic in the middle of winter.

"I don't want the map," he said softly. "I *want* to keep Hayley safe."

Harriet stopped walking and frowned. "What do you mean? I don't understand."

"Alex is worried that if the killer knows Hayley has the map he'll go after her to get it," Solly explained. "Otherwise, why kill Holden?"

Despite the warm sun, icy fear brought up goose bumps on Harriet's arms. "Oh my God. We have to get to the hotel." Harriet pulled her hand free from Alex's hold and broke into a run.

Alex kissed his brief fantasy of taking a long, leisurely shower with Harriet goodbye. He followed her up to Mermaid Cottage with Solly on his heels.

"I don't think the Tiger will carry all three of

us so I'll meet you at the hotel," Solly said, heading to his own lanai. "I'll head there as soon as I clean up. " He disappeared inside Venus.

Alex heard the water running in the shower as soon as he stepped inside the cottage. He went to the kitchen for water while he waited for Harriet to clean up and tried not to think about her standing naked in the shower with soap and water running over her smooth, lean muscles. He was so caught up in the pleasant image he didn't hear the water shut off.

"Shower's all yours." Harriet stood in the kitchen doorway wrapped in a towel. "Hurry, please. Hayley should be fine, but I'm worried just the same. We were supposed to go back to the amusement park this morning. On the days I do something with them they wait for me in the hotel lobby."

"She's with her friends, right?"

Harriet nodded. "They're inseparable. The hotel keeps an eye on them until whoever's turn it is to take them arrives. We'll be early so I expect they'll still be having breakfast in their suite."

Harriet knew she was babbling but she couldn't seem to stop herself. Alex stopped in front of her on his way to the shower and clasped both her arms in his warm, strong hands, pulling her close.

"Hayley will be fine, Harriet," he said firmly. "We'll be there in twenty minutes. Call Fox and tell him there's been a change in the morning plans. He's going to go to the amusement park with you and your girls today while I talk to some people again. I want an extra set of eyes on Hayley."

"Okay." Harriet allowed herself to be held for a long moment. She took a deep breath and pushed away from Alex. "I'm okay. The girls are surrounded by people at the hotel. I doubt that anyone would dare to kidnap or hurt Hayley with so many people around. I'll get dressed and call Fox."

She wished she hadn't thought of kidnapping. Fisting her hands to stop their trembling, she turned and ran into the bedroom to dress.

CHAPTER TWENTY

As it turned out, Harriet and Alex arrived at the hotel in under fifteen minutes with Solly right behind them. Harriet's anxiety over the possibility of the murderer going after Hayley had grown during the quick ride from her cottage to the hotel.

If anything happened to the little girl it would be Harriet's fault for not looking after her better. She had thought of the resort as a safe haven for the kids, never even considered that danger could lurk unseen. Her chest tightened until it was difficult to draw a breath.

When he pulled up in front of the hotel lobby, Harriet didn't wait for Alex to park the bike, but jumped off as soon as he stopped and ran inside.

The lobby was humming with activity even at

the early hour. There always seemed to be an even mix of guests–those who looked at their time on the island as an opportunity to escape the hectic pace of their lives on the mainland–to relax, sleep late, and be leisurely–and those guests who didn't want to miss a single moment of fun activity.

Harriet was happy to see the latter group of guests up and about, making the most of their vacation time on the island. Lots of people milling about meant lots of eyes if the murderer had tried anything.

Large urns filled with bright tropical flowers had been placed strategically to help direct traffic flow. Potted green palms blended with mango, papaya, and starfruit trees provided a modicum of privacy around the half dozen seating areas scattered throughout the lobby.

Solly had done an outstanding job with the flowers and greenery, but she wouldn't have expected anything less. If there were two things her best friend truly understood it was gardening and design. The resort was the perfect venue to show off his skills and artistry.

The lobby ceiling rose the hotel's full two stories, giving it a spacious feel and providing plenty of natural light for the growing plants. Tempered glass, manufactured to withstand the fiercest hurricane, filled the exterior wall. The ground level accordion glass doors had been pushed back, opening the lobby to the fresh sea breeze.

Harriet recognized Elliot Winston standing next to the coffee bar, talking with two teenage boys she assumed were his sons while he waited for the latte machine to finish hissing. She turned away before he could catch her eye. After his callous attitude toward Holden's death the night before she was afraid that speaking politely would be beyond her capabilities.

An older couple dressed for the beach grabbed thick, turquoise and white striped towels, fresh fruit, and several waters and stuffed it all into one of the large beach bags the resort provided. Harriet noted the empty complimentary sunscreen shelf and made a mental note to mention it to the desk clerk.

Alex joined her as she headed toward the front desk to speak to the clerk.

Fox was already waiting in the lobby with a cup of coffee, chatting up one of the desk clerks and looking amazingly rested for the few hours of sleep she knew he'd managed.

"Morning, boss," Fox drawled. He pushed away from the counter. "What's up?"

"I want you to escort Harriet and her three girls around the island today," Alex answered. "Don't let them out of your sight."

Fox's eyebrows went up. He shot Harriet a curious look. "Any particular reason?"

"Yes. I think our killer is going to attempt to nab a little girl called Hayley, or at the very least, try to steal Hayley's fanny pack. When he does you can identify him. But, Fox?" Alex stopped speaking, moved closer to his assistant, and lowered his voice.

"Protecting those girls is your first priority. If it comes down to keeping them safe and letting the killer get away you let the killer go. He won't get far. Understood?"

Fox looked wounded. "What kind of man do you take me for, Alex? Of course I'll protect Harry and the girls. Where are the little ladies?"

"Still having breakfast in their suite. Harriet and I are headed up there now to get them. Wait for us down here. We shouldn't be long."

"How can I help?" Solly asked from behind them.

Alex turned to him. "Keep your eyes open for anyone hanging around the lobby who doesn't behave like a normal guest. I'm guessing you spend a fair amount of time here looking after the greenery so you'll have a feel for someone who acts out of place. Let me get the girls settled with Fox, then you and I can start hunting our killer."

Harriet was already halfway up the wide staircase that led to the second floor suites when Alex caught up with her.

"Fox is going to stick with you and the girls today while Solly and I talk a second time with a few people and see if we can narrow down our list. I don't believe our killer will try anything with both of you watching out for the girls."

She didn't question why Alex wanted Fox with her instead of Solly. Her friend was a gardener, not a trained law enforcement officer.

The hotel's second floor had a wide central hallway with two-bedroom suites off each side, twenty in total, and large open windows at the far end to let in the light and cross breeze. The gentle buzz of voices drifted up from the lobby.

Just another normal day at the resort.

Harriet's sandals echoed slightly on the hallway's light bamboo floor. She hurried past small tables set outside each door, topped with vases filled with fresh flowers.

The pale teal walls held large paintings hung between the suites. Like the murals in her office building, the paintings depicted island scenes and were painted by local artists.

Stopping by a painting of fishermen hauling their brightly painted boats onto a beach, she knocked briefly on the door next to it, then entered without waiting for an answer. Alex followed right behind her. The hotel maid assigned to the suite looked up in surprise and shut off her vacuum cleaner.

"Miss Harriet, what are you doing here?"

Harriet searched her memory for the maid's name and came up with it.

"It's Hilda, right? I'm here to take the girls to the amusement park." She looked around the suite's living/dining area but saw no sign of the girls. A ball of icy fear formed in the pit of her stomach.

"Where are they?" she asked.

Hilda's dark eyebrows knotted together. Her turquoise maid uniform showed off beautiful deep, dark skin that reminded Harriet of ebony wood. Hilda's eyes, a startling green that looked too bright to be natural, looked confused.

"They went to meet you, Miss. They told me you were meeting them in the lobby early today and they wanted to go down by themselves. They know the way. I've been bringing them down every morning and usually they're leading the way. They like to get something from the snack bar even though they've usually just had breakfast." She smiled indulgently.

"How long ago did they leave?" snapped Alex. He stepped in front of Harriet, who still stood in the open doorway. Hearing the bark in his voice, the maid took a step back. Suppressing a sigh, Alex made himself take a friendlier approach.

"Hilda, I'm Alex Hayes, the director of security for the resort." He held out his hand to shake. "I try to get to know all the resort employees but we haven't had a chance to meet yet. Unfortunately we don't have time to get to know each other right now."

Hilda visibly relaxed and shook his hand. "What would the security director be wanting with those three? They've done nothing wrong, I'm sure. Not them. They are the sweetest little girls."

The maid was no fool. Alex decided to tell her the truth. The more people on the lookout for the three girls the better.

"We think someone might be after the girls. They weren't waiting in the lobby for Harriet. We were just there."

Hilda's hand pressed against her chest. "Oh, Lordy. What would someone want to hurt those little angels for?"

"Did they say where they might be going?" Harriet asked. "Or say anything that might help us find them?"

"They was whispering about looking for a treasure. I thought you was maybe taking them on a scavenger hunt today. They seemed very excited about it."

Alex exchanged a look with Harriet. "Can you tell me exactly when they left the suite?"

Hilda checked her wrist unit. "At least a half hour, maybe forty-five minutes ago. I remember feeling surprised that Miss Harriet would want to get such an early start. At the time I figured it must be a long scavenger hunt."

"We'd better get some people looking for them." Alex turned to Harriet. He could tell by the paleness of her face that she was assuming the worst.

Hilda whipped off her apron. "I want to help look. I've grown quite fond of those three. Besides, those little girls have had enough trouble in their short lives. I don't want anything to happen to them."

"Neither do we, Hilda. Neither do we. Your help is welcome. The more bodies looking the faster we'll find them." Alex took Harriet's arm and turned her toward the hall.

"They decided to look for the treasure on their own," he said quietly, so Hilda wouldn't hear. "They left on their own. No one took them."

Harriet understood that Alex was telling her not to worry, but the greasy ball of fear clawing at her gut didn't ease any.

Hilda locked the door to the girls' suite and followed them down to the lobby. Alex went straight to the front desk where Fox waited off to the side, talking with Solly and enjoying what Harriet assumed was a fresh cup of coffee. They stopped talking when she joined them and looked at her expectantly.

"They're gone," she told them both. Fox swore and deposited the coffee in a nearby trash can. "What's the plan?"

Harriet shook her head. The worry and dread filling her made it difficult to think clearly. "I don't know. We have to find them."

Alex waited impatiently for the desk clerk to finish giving directions to the marina to a mother with three teenage children eagerly hanging on the counter. As soon as the woman left with the teens, Alex nabbed the clerk.

"We're looking for the three orphans who've been hanging with Harriet. They would have been in the lobby between a half hour to an hour ago. Did you see them?"

The desk clerk, a handsome young island man, smiled. "Of course. You mean Hayley, Dorian, and Amber Lee, right? They picked up waters and snacks about–" he checked his desk unit–"about forty-five minutes ago, I'd say."

Harriet left Fox and Solly and pushed up to

the counter next to Alex. "I thought you were supposed to be keeping an eye on them."

The clerk immediately looked defensive. "The maid usually brings them down to meet you, Miss Harriet. When Hilda didn't accompany them I assumed other plans had been made. Then the girls told me you were meeting them in front of the hotel this morning for something special. I had no reason to doubt them." He suddenly looked worried.

"Is there a problem?" he asked.

"Yes. The girls are missing." Harriet took a deep breath and tried to calm her racing heart. It wasn't right to take her fears out on the clerk.

"It isn't your fault Darrin. I'm sorry I snapped at you. I'm worried about them."

Alex stepped away from the desk and strode to the center of the lobby.

"Listen up, everybody," he said loudly. He waited until he had the attention of every guest and employee.

"We have a situation. Three young girls are missing. One is caramel skinned, one is a redhead, and one is of Asian descent. They'll be together. Did any of you happen to see them in the lobby this morning, between one half and one hour ago?"

A portly, elderly gentleman sitting in one of

the seating areas reading raised his hand. "I saw them," he said.

"Did you speak with them?" Alex asked. Harriet hurried over to stand beside him.

The man smiled. "Certainly did. They were excited. Talking about going to look for something. I was at the food bar waiting for my morning espresso and they were collecting snacks. The Asian girl asked me to get three power bars for them. They were too high for her to reach," he explained. "Very polite, too. Nice little girls. Raised proper, unlike a lot of today's youth."

"That confirms it," Harriet told Alex quietly. "You were right. They went to search for the treasure on their own. We have to go to the amusement park, Alex. The X on the map was by the lagoon at the top of what's now the water slide."

Alex grabbed her hand before she could run off and pulled her to his side.

"Wait." He raised his voice again so everyone could hear him.

"If any of you should see the girls while you're out and about today please contact either the security office or the hotel's front desk and let them know where you saw them. Whoever's on duty will contact us immediately."

"Do you need help searching?"

Harriet turned and saw Elliot Winston

standing behind her with his two sons. She didn't want Elliot's help. They didn't know the killer's identity, and Elliot had been at the circus when Holden was murdered. For all she knew, Elliot could be the killer.

Fortunately Alex was thinking along the same lines.

"Thank you, Mr. Winston, but for the moment we have staff to help. We would appreciate it though, if you could keep an eye out for the girls while you enjoy the resort today and contact us if you see them."

"Will do. Come on, boys. Let's grab a cart and take a trip up to the coves. We'll look for the girls there." He headed out of the hotel with his sons on his heels looking like a man on a mission.

"Alex. He completely ignored you."

"I know." Alex shook his head. "There's nothing we can do, Harriet. If it eases your mind any, I don't think Winston is our killer. Not unless his sons are involved. They're always with him."

Harriet didn't like it, but she knew there was nothing she could do. She put Elliot Winston out of her mind.

By that time, Darrin had rallied a dozen hotel employees including Hilda, and gathered them near the front desk. Alex split them into groups of two and assigned each group a different area of the resort to search. They could cover more ground if he sent them out solo, but they were safer traveling in pairs if they ran into the killer.

Even though he agreed with Harriet that the lagoon at the top of the water slide was the most likely place to look for the girls, he couldn't rule out the possibility that they'd become sidetracked and head in another direction. They were young children after all, and children had notoriously short attention spans.

"We'll take the Road Hog," he told Fox and Solly as they headed for the door. "It's faster, and when we find the girls we'll need a vehicle large enough for everyone."

"Shouldn't Fox and I search too?" Solly asked. "More eyes and all that?"

"No. I want you both with me, just in case we find the girls and a situation develops." He didn't want to say the word "hostage" in Harriet's hearing.

"You know something I don't," Fox accused as they left the hotel. "What's this about? Why would our murderer go after three little girls?"

"I'll fill you in on the way to the amusement park. Let's go."

CHAPTER TWENTY-ONE

Harriet appreciated the power of the Road Hog. If she had been forced to take one of the resort carts to the amusement park she would've been beside herself with frustration at the slow speed.

She said a silent prayer that they would find the girls safe and unharmed. She wasn't only worried about the murderer catching up to them, there were snakes and biting insects and other dangers in the jungle.

Cassie had told her about a small group of protected jungle panthers who lived in the mountains. What if a panther decided to hunt near the amusement park? The girls would be defenseless against a large predator.

Even if the girls managed to avoid the jungle's

dangers, the rocks around the lagoon could be slippery. Parts of the lagoon were well over the girls' heads in depth, especially near the foot of the upper waterfall. The girls had only recently learned how to float. Why hadn't she insisted that they learn to swim?

There were so many ways for a young child to get hurt or even killed.

She felt Solly squeeze her hand and realized her hands were shaking. They sat in the Hog's middle seat. Fox had sat in the front with Alex so Alex could fill him in about the treasure map.

"They're going to be okay, Harry," Solly told her quietly. He always did have a knack for reading her mind.

"I don't know what I'll do if–"

"They haven't been gone long enough to get into serious trouble," he said firmly. "We'll find them. And when we do we'll both read them the riot act about the dangers of roaming around a tropical island on their own. And *then* we'll preach fire and brimstone about not letting their elders know where they were going."

Harriet tried to smile but couldn't. "If anything happens to any one of those girls I'm going to shut down the orphan program, Solly. I can't take this kind of worry. At least the adult guests are responsible for themselves and their children. I'm responsible for every one of those orphans. *Every one.* If anything happens . . . " She knew she was repeating herself but couldn't seem to stop.

Alex caught her eye in the Hog's rearview mirror. "We'll find the girls, I promise. I don't want to hear any more talk about giving up on your orphan program. It's early days yet–you're still working out the kinks, Harriet."

Fox turned in his seat and grinned at her. "Not only that, you have the entire resort invested in the success of the program. They look forward to the orphans being here. Your co-workers will run you off the island if you try to shut the program down now."

Solly gave Alex a thoughtful look. "Doesn't it seem like there are a lot of orphans involved in this mess? Harriet's orphans, Holden was an orphan–and there are several other orphans with the circus. Just out of curiosity, was Davis an orphan?"

"That's an interesting point. I don't know about Davis. I didn't look back that far. I'll check on him when I get back to my office."

Alex pulled up to the amusement park gate and looked at his wrist unit.

"The park doesn't open for another half hour. The girls aren't here yet."

Solly shook his head and smirked at Alex. "A closed gate won't mean anything if the girls are determined to get into the park, Alex. When Harry and I were young we found ways to get into all kinds of places we weren't supposed to be. Some of them would give you goosebumps. Trust me, if this is where the girls were headed they're in there."

Harriet jumped out of the Hog. She knew exactly which goosebump-y place Solly was referring to. One particularly cold winter night when they couldn't find shelter they had climbed through the broken basement window of an abandoned mortuary. The place had been so spooky that neither of them had slept a wink.

The amusement park gate hadn't been designed to seriously keep people out. Bending over, she easily slid between two horizontal rails and waited on the inside for the others to join her.

The park had security cameras and a twenty-four hour watchman. The park manager had also placed hidden kill switches on all of the rides. Someone might be able to figure out how to start a ride, but it would shut down within thirty seconds and also send a silent alarm to Braxton Holliday's quarters as well as the security office.

"Wait up." Alex quickly stepped through the gate and joined Harriet. "We'll search together."

"They'll be at the water slide, I'm sure of it," she told him again. It took a real effort to keep her voice calm. The urge to break into a run was strong, but she knew that the murderer could already be in the park following the girls. If he was, some degree of stealth was probably a better option.

"Sorry folks, no one's allowed in the amusement park until it officially opens. Only another hour." The guard drew himself up, giving Harriet and the men a stern look, then relaxed when he recognized Harriet.

"Oh, it's you, Harry. I wasn't expecting to see anyone this early. Where's your little posse? You really shouldn't be here, you know. Rules is rules, even for management."

Belatedly, the security guard recognized Alex. He frowned, clearly confused. "Mr. Hayes? What's going on?"

"Sandy, have you seen the three little girls I've been escorting around all week?" Harriet asked. "They're missing. We thought they might be here."

Sandy, a slim older man of mixed descent who took his job of guarding the amusement park very seriously, pursed his lips.

"Oh dear. I hope those little girls are okay." He

shook his head. "I haven't seen them. No one's been here this morning that shouldn't be."

Harriet thanked him and started to walk off, but stopped and walked back when she heard Solly ask Sandy who *had* been there.

"That red haired writer from the mainland was here earlier," Sandy replied. "She had permission from Cassie to re-con-struct the murder at the water slide and wanted to check it out without bothering the other guests. She's gonna write a script for the dinner theater, she told me. Wanted to get a feel for how it would have happened."

"Fiona Sprite was here? Is she still here?" Harriet had told the script writer she could only write about old murders. Why would Fiona be researching Davis's murder? Unless . . . unless she planned to write a story for one of the mainland tabloids and had lied to Cassie about it.

Harriet clamped her jaw in anger. The next time she saw Fiona she and the writer were going to sort a few things out. Either that or Fiona would be finding herself on the next shuttle off the island.

"I don't know if she's still here or not." Sandy shrugged. "I didn't see her leave, but I haven't been back by the slide in a while. She could still be there. Or I coulda missed her if I was on one path and she took the other one."

He scratched his ear. "I guess I coulda missed the girls too, come to think of it."

"Thanks, Sandy. Give me a call if you see Miss Sprite leave, would you please?" Alex gave Sandy his link number. "Appreciate it."

Sandy nodded and ambled off toward the food court.

"Miss Sprite certainly gets around," Solly said with a sideways glance toward Harriet. He knew that set of her jaw. He hadn't seen it often in all the years they'd been friends, but when Harry clenched her jaw like that he knew someone was about to get blasted. He suspected Miss Fiona Sprite was in for it.

"I've told her that she can't write about recent murders because it could potentially leave the resort open to lawsuits," Harriet muttered after Sandy was out of earshot. "Apparently I didn't make myself clearly understood."

"Never mind Sprite now," Alex told her. "You can deal with her later. You heard Sandy–he could have missed the girls as well as Miss Sprite if they took the path he wasn't on."

Worry quickly replaced Harriet's anger. They needed to find the girls and put them someplace safe. After they'd been found she'd contact Cassie and tell her Fiona wasn't working out. Cassie wouldn't question her opinion. She'd send Fiona packing and find another script writer. Problem solved.

The park felt unusually quiet without the roller coaster clacking overhead and the music from the merry-go-round in the background. Small colorful birds twittered and chirped high in the trees and shrubs and green geckos darted after insects. The scent of flowers and earth were more noticeable without the smells from the food court to compete with them.

As they walked toward the water slide Harriet tried to imagine what the area had been like before the resort, back during the time when pirates actually visited the island and possibly buried their stolen loot.

It wasn't difficult to picture. Douglas Wade had been careful to preserve as much of the island's natural wilderness as possible, integrating the resort into it instead of dozing the island to make room for the resort's buildings.

She caught glimpses of the thin silver ribbon of the stream that cascaded down the mountain in a series of falls that ended in the lagoon. That same ribbon of fresh water would have attracted passing ships.

Hardened men used to a life at sea once walked where she walked, carrying or rolling wooden barrels to fill with drinking water for their ships.

Had they also bathed in the lagoon or did cleanliness not matter to them?

"You've never been one to beat your chops, but you're unusually quiet, Harry. Penny for your thoughts?"

Chagrinned by the fact that she'd been caught daydreaming for the last few minutes, Harriet gave Fox a rueful smile.

"I was thinking about the pirates who used the island for fresh water and fruit and possibly hiding their loot. I, ah, I was wondering if they ever bothered to bathe when they had the chance." She felt her face heat and knew she was blushing.

"Hmmm." Fox gave the question some serious thought as he walked at her side.

"I'm going with no," he finally answered. "They were used to going months or even a year at a time without bathing at sea because they couldn't spare the fresh water and few of them actually knew how to swim. Plus, for a long time people believed bathing to be an unhealthy pastime.

"Besides, just think about how much more terrifying it would be to face down a stinky pirate with a dirty face and ratty hair and missing teeth compared to one who smelled sweet with clean shiny hair?"

He smiled when a laugh burbled out Harriet. "That's better."

The path opened to the shallow lagoon at the foot of the water slide. Harriet scanned the benches set around the water but saw no sign of the girls or Fiona Sprite.

She felt relief at having missed Fiona, admitting to herself that she really didn't care for the writer and would have resented her presence, especially after the way Fiona had come on to Alex the previous night.

"According to Leonard, the X on the map was near the lagoon at the top of the water slide," she told the others, putting Fiona out of her thoughts until she could speak with Cassie about her.

"The girls know where the lagoon is because it sits beside the entrance to the slide. I warned them to stay away from it because of the slippery rocks, but they weren't interested in it at the time anyway. They just wanted to slide."

Harriet headed up the steps with Solly behind her. Alex and Fox were already halfway up the steps ahead of her. When she reached the top, both men were staring at three small pairs of sandals lined up neatly under the tall chair the slide attendant sat in when not assisting guests.

"Those belong to the girls. They're here." Harriet cupped her hands around her mouth. "Hayley! Amber Lee! Dorian!" She listened for an answering shout but all she could hear was the water splashing over the fall and against the slides.

"Which side of the lagoon was the X on the map on?" asked Alex.

"Uh." Harriet tried to recall holding the map over her head in the boat. "I can't think. Left. No, it was on the right. It doesn't matter, Alex. The girls could have easily gotten confused and headed in either direction."

"Okay. We split up. Fox, you take Solly and search the right side of the lagoon. Harriet and I will take the left. Take your time and be thorough. Check about fifteen feet into the jungle but don't lose sight of each other. It can get thick fast and it's easy to get lost. I think the girls would have been more likely to stick close to the edge of the lagoon. The jungle can be scary."

The thought that the girls could have wandered into the jungle made Harriet's breath catch. If they were in the jungle the search would be much more difficult and would need more people. *Please let us find them,* she prayed silently.

She was glad she'd worn trainers and not sandals. The rocks on the edge of the lagoon were worn smooth and rounded and took some effort to balance on. She searched the pockets of sand between the rocks at the edge of the water, looking for small footprints or any other sign that the girls had passed that way, while Alex searched just inside the edge of the jungle's thick growth.

The lagoon was longer than it was wide and irregular in shape. Trees arched over the water in several places, trailing thick vines and making it difficult to walk the water's edge. The closer they drew to the waterfall the deeper the water became, the bottom scoured out by thousands or millions of years of water washing away the soil.

"Anything?" Alex asked. Harriet could just make out his tan chinos through the undergrowth to her left.

"No. Oh, Alex, I was so sure this is where they came. What if I'm wrong? I don't know where else to look for them."

"Trust your instincts, Harriet. The man who helped them reach the snack bars in the lobby this morning said they were going treasure hunting. This is where the treasure is supposed to be, according to Hayley's map. Your girls are not only clever, they're smart. We'll find them."

Fox interrupted their conversation with a shout.

"Got a footprint over here! Definitely one of

the girls! Headed that way." He pointed toward the narrow waterfall that fed the lagoon.

"Good work!" Alex called across. "We'll meet you at the waterfall. Come on, Harriet. With any luck our intrepid treasure hunters will be holed up just ahead."

CHAPTER TWENTY-TWO

The waterfall at the head of the lagoon grew louder the closer Harriet and Alex got to it until it thundered so loudly it made talking nearly impossible. Silvered water cascaded off the scoured rock surfaces and entered the lagoon in a boiling white froth of bubbles.

Cool spray from the waterfall rolled off the lush green vegetation on either side of the falls in a constant drip, drip, drip that filled the air as effectively as a rain shower, turning every surface dark and slippery and treacherous.

Solly and Fox had reached the falls on the other side and were pointing to something on the ground. Fox pulled his link and made a call.

Alex pulled his link from his pocket, spoke for

a minute, and replaced it. He leaned close to Harriet's ear.

"Fox says there's another footprint where he's pointing. It appears to lead into the waterfall."

"Where are they?" Harriet shouted. She scanned the steep wall of mountain in front of them. Surely the girls hadn't tried to scale its slippery face. She half expected to see their small bodies crumpled at its base. Or god forbid, caught beneath the falls, drowned and tumbling against the rocks.

The thought that they might have veered into the jungle from that point made her shudder. Surviving the jungle on their own would take a miracle. Harriet shook her head in an effort to dislodge the morbid images in her mind's eye.

From the corner of her eye she saw Solly disappear, as if he'd walked straight into the waterfall. What was he thinking? The water was going to sweep him under. He'd die just as surely as the girls had died.

Her heart seized with fear. She had almost lost Solly not too long ago. She couldn't bear to go through that again.

She watched the roiling water at the base of the falls, waiting for a glimpse of her friend's body. She felt her link vibrate in her pocket and ignored it. There was no one she wanted to speak with at that moment. She'd just lost three little girls and her best friend.

She barely noticed Alex on his link again, most likely setting up body recovery from the falls or else a search in the jungle.

The growth was so thick and lush she couldn't see even a yard beyond the lagoon's edge. What if the jungle cats were nearby and had smelled the girls? The large predators were every bit as fierce and lethal as the saltwater crocs in the mangrove swamp.

"Solly has Dorian and Amber Lee."

"What?" Harriet grabbed Alex's arm. "Where are they?"

Alex didn't answer. He pulled free and carefully stepped closer to the waterfall. Finding a foothold, he pressed right up against the rock face, then turned and beckoned to Harriet.

"Hold your breath," he shouted in her ear when she joined him. "We're going in." He grabbed her hand firmly and pulled her into the waterfall.

Harriet barely had time to fill her lungs before she found herself buried in a solid wall of water. It pressed down on her head and shoulders with unbelievable power. She hugged the rock face as best she could, resisting the fall's efforts to sweep her off her feet and into the lagoon.

Her right foot slipped and she stumbled. She felt the powerful falls grab her and push her away from the rock face. She opened her mouth to scream but it filled with water.

Out of air, Harriet felt her hand begin to slip from Alex's. He couldn't fight the force of the water, couldn't hold onto her. Would she be beaten against the rocks hiding at the base of the falls?

She felt Alex immediately tighten his grip. For a moment she felt him war against the water slamming against her body and didn't see how he could win, then he yanked and pulled her after him. Suddenly she was free of the water and standing in the entrance of a wide, shallow cave.

She coughed and gasped for air, blinked the water from her eyes, and looked around anxiously for the girls.

Sunlight filtered through the curtain of water blocking the entrance. The cave felt cool but the dark dirt floor seemed dry. There were signs of digging in the center of the cave. A small shovel had been tossed to one side. Much to her surprise, the falls didn't sound as loud inside the cave.

Solly stood at the opposite, outer edge of the chamber, a grim expression on his face. She could see a narrow gap between the falls and the rock face behind him. That explained how the girls had accessed the cave.

Amber Lee and Dorian sat in the dirt, huddled together against the back wall of the shallow space, their frightened faces streaked with tears.

As soon as Harriet spied the girls, she dropped to her knees and opened her arms. They ran to her and she scooped them both close.

"Are you all right?" she asked them. "Are you hurt?" She tried to inspect their faces and look them over but they clung tightly to her neck.

When she looked up she saw that Solly had retreated from the cave. In a moment of clarity she realized the girls didn't know any of the men. Solly's appearance had frightened them, otherwise he would have carried them from the cave himself.

Leave it to Solly to understand that. Her friend really was quite marvelous.

Alex knelt beside her and put a hand on her back. Harriet suspected that he too had realized that the sight of strange men would frighten the girls.

"Dorian? Amber Lee? My name is Alex. You can trust me. Harriet and I are very good friends. We're here to take you back to the hotel, but Harriet can't carry both of you. Would it be all right if I take one of you out of here?"

He watched the girls look at each other and silently communicate something. After a long minute, Dorian loosened her grip on Harriet's neck and gave him a shy nod. He wondered how many grown men were part of their lives and felt his throat tighten at the gesture of trust. He suspected they'd had very few positive experiences with adult males in their short lives.

Scooping Dorian up, he whispered to her to hold tight, then took Harriet's hand and helped her to her feet, her other arm still tightly holding onto Amber Lee who clung to her like a baby monkey.

Harriet was relieved to find that leaving the cave by the entrance Solly and Fox had found was much easier than the way she and Alex had used. Once outside the group made their way down the lagoon until they'd put some distance between themselves and the roar of the falls.

Harriet's arm felt as if it was going to fall off by the time they stopped. She deposited Amber Lee on a rock beside Dorian and shook out the pain.

"Oof," she said with a smile. "You're getting to be a big girl, Amber Lee."

She was frantic to find out where Hayley was, but knew Dorian and Amber Lee had been traumatized and needed to be treated gently. It wouldn't help the situation for them to see her own fear.

The three men had stepped back slightly and were letting her take the lead with the girls. Ignoring the damp dirt, she dropped to her knees in front of Dorian and Amber Lee and took each one's hand.

"I was worried sick about you," she began. "I'm very, *very* glad to see that you're both okay, but where is Hayley? Please tell me she didn't get swept into the waterfall."

She almost cried out with relief when one dark head and one bright red head both shook no.

"Where is she then? Why isn't she with you?" She watched Dorian glance at Amber Lee out of the corner of her eye. Amber Lee gave her head a slight shake. Dorian shrugged a shoulder and said nothing.

So. The girls were holding back. They had to have a good reason to do so. She knew they both loved Hayley. She watched them while she thought.

Hayley wouldn't have left her friends behind. Something had happened to split them up.

Something or *someone*.

Had the killer taken Hayley? Harriet schooled her face to not show the worry and fear coursing through her. How was she going to get the information they needed from the girls?

Fortunately inspiration struck. She had used a game to break the ice with a couple of shy girls in the first group of orphans who visited the resort. With them she had kept the game light and silly, but maybe she could use it now to get the information they needed.

"Okaaay," she said slowly. "Let's play the guessing game. Do you know the rules?" Amber Lee and Dorian both looked interested. They shook their heads.

"If I guess right you have to say or nod yes. If I'm wrong you shake your head. I only get three wrong guesses, then it's your turn. Ready?"

Both girls nodded and Harriet felt a small surge of relief. It was going to work. She tapped her chin with a finger and acted like she was deep in thought. Then she pointed the finger at Dorian.

"You and Hayley decided to search for the treasure this morning, so you left the hotel early."

Two nods.

"We'll talk about that later. Let me see . . . you somehow got to the amusement park and hiked to the second waterfall because you thought that's where the treasure was buried."

Two nods. "We took a cart," Dorian said, then

rolled her lips together as if to keep more words from popping out.

A cart? How did they–? Harriet shook her head. It wasn't important at the moment. Finding Hayley was all that mattered.

"Okay. Let's see. You left the hotel to look for the treasure. You came to the waterfall because that's where the X is on Hayley's map." She looked at the far end of the lagoon where the girls had left their shoes at the top of the water slide. Why would they split up?

The only answer she came up with spiked her fear.

"You met someone, either at the water slide or here by the second waterfall." Dorian's lips trembled and her eyes filled with tears. Amber Lee gave a curt nod.

"Did you know him? Had you seen him around the resort?"

Dorian nodded and Amber Lee shook her head vehemently.

Harriet frowned at the girls. "What? How can the answer be a yes *and* a no? I don't understand."

"We know *her*," Amber Lee corrected. "She's your friend."

Stunned, Harriet rocked back on her heels. "My friend? Who is she?"

The girls both shook their heads.

"We can't tell you," Dorian said. "She told us that she'd hurt Hayley if we tried to get help." Her eyes filled with tears again.

"We're supposed to wait in the cave until she comes back for us."

Now that Dorian was talking, Amber Lee's lips loosened up as well and the words tumbled out.

"She followed us to the water slide and took Hayley's map and made us hike to the cave behind the waterfall. She found a box buried in the dirt and put it in her backpack. Then she took Hayley and told us we had to stay in the cave until she came back for us and if we tried to go for help she'd know and she'd hurt Hayley, maybe dump her in the ocean."

"But we can't tell you her name," Dorian added, "because Hayley can't swim. I don't want her to hurt Hayley." She began to sob. Amber Lee put her arm around Dorian's shoulders.

Harriet leaned in close and gently wiped the tears from Dorian's cheeks with her thumbs. "Shhhh. We aren't going to let anything happen to Hayley. You see those big strong men behind me?" Dorian peered over her shoulder and nodded.

"They are good men, real life heroes, and they're going to help us rescue Hayley."

"P-promise?"

"I promise." Harriet released Dorian's face and stood.

"I know who we're looking for," she told Alex. All three men looked at her expectantly.

"Who is a recent stranger on the resort, an orphan, and was with us when Hayley found the map? I'm willing to bet that the two dead men and Fiona Sprite all came from the same orphanage."

"Sprite? Who's that?" Fox asked.

"You haven't met her yet," Alex explained. "Cassie hired her to write some new scripts for the dinner theatre." He gave the girls a thoughtful look, then turned his gaze back to Harriet.

"But you overheard two men talking behind the circus cabana."

"I heard two low voices. Think back to last night when I introduced you to Fiona. Remember how low and husky her voice was?"

Alex nodded. "Okay. Yeah. Hangs together. The orphanage would explain how they all knew each other. Madame Zaza said we were looking for a woman, then she changed her mind."

"Yeah. I have a theory on that, too, but I'll save it for after we find Hayley." She leaned down to look both girls in the eyes.

"Did Miss Sprite say anything that would help us find where she took Hayley?"

"She dug up Hayley's treasure," Dorian said sadly. "We saw her find the box."

"Did she open it?" Solly asked, curious.

"No. She laughed. Then she said she had what she came for and it was all hers and it was time to get off the island."

The three men looked at one another.

"There are only two ways off the island," Solly pointed out.

"Right. Boat or air shuttle." Alex lifted Dorian onto his shoulders. She squealed and grabbed fistfuls of hair. Alex bit back a grimace.

"Let's go. Fox, can you take Amber Lee? Amber Lee, this is my partner, Fox. We can look for Hayley faster if you let him carry you out of here."

Amber Lee looked to Harriet for confirmation. At Harriet's nod she lifted her arms toward Fox. He swung her onto his shoulders with a "jiggity-boo, look at you," that made both girls giggle.

They made the trip back to the Road Hog in much less time than it took them to find the waterfall cave. Once everyone was strapped in, Alex wasted no time alerting the search teams to be on the lookout for a red-haired woman suspected of kidnapping Hayley.

He brought the girls back to the hotel where they were deposited in the care of their waiting maid. Hilda cried when she saw them and cursed when she realized Hayley was still missing.

The girls made Harriet promise to bring Hayley to them as soon as she was found before they'd let her leave. As soon as the door to the girls' suite closed behind them, Harriet whirled on Alex and grabbed his arm.

"If that bitch has harmed a hair on Hayley's head I swear I'm going to hurt her bad. Just warning you."

Alex gave her a hard, quick kiss. "Let's make sure she doesn't get the chance." He was on his link with the air pad and speaking with Leonard at the marina before they reached the hotel lobby.

CHAPTER TWENTY-THREE

When Alex and Harriet descended into the lobby, Alex immediately searched for Solly and Fox. He spied the men waiting for them by the front desk. Elliot Winston and his two boys had returned and were apparently trying to wring information from Fox.

"Winston." Alex gave Winston a curt nod to dismiss him, but Winston pushed into Alex's personal space instead of taking the hint.

"We saw you take the little redhead and one of her friends upstairs," Winston said eagerly. "Where did you find them? There's still a girl missing, isn't there? Do you think the murderer got her too? What we can do to help?"

Alex felt Harriet stiffen beside him and moved to place himself between her and the clueless

Winston. It took effort to keep the irritation from his face. While he appreciated the man's desire to help, the last thing he needed was a gung-ho amateur and his two clueless sons bumbling about and possibly putting Hayley in more danger than she was already in.

Added to that, Alex agreed with Harriet's assessment of Winston–while the man probably considered himself a do-gooder, at heart he was only looking for more gossip fodder to share around his office water cooler.

He decided it was time to stop pussy-footing around and gave Winston a stern look.

"We appreciate the help you've given us, Mr. Winston, but we have the situation under control. The best thing you can do now is to stay out of our way and let us do our jobs. Return to enjoying your holiday. Please."

He heard Winston grumble something about ungrateful so-and-so's as he turned away and jerked his head toward the doors, a signal that Fox and Solly should follow him and Harriet outside.

"Boss?"

"Outside." He didn't want Winston to hear what he had to say.

"I want you and Solly to head to the air pad," he told Fox, once they were out of earshot.

"Search it thoroughly, including any shuttles on the ground and the surrounding area. Search any hidey-hole small enough to hide a little girl. Harriet and I will check the marina."

"You really think the woman will hold on to a hostage?" Fox asked. "Dragging the kid along will only slow her down." He winced when he saw the look on Harriet's face.

"Sorry, Harry. I didn't think before I spoke."

Harriet shook her head. "I'm not stupid, Tarbell. I know that Fiona has already killed two men. What's one more death–and an easy target at that. Let's just find her before she can hurt Hayley."

Alex dragged his hand over his face. The lack of sleep was beginning to really wear on him.

"I don't know what Miss Sprite will do at this point. We don't know enough about her. Why didn't she just leave all three girls in the cave? That would have made the most sense to me. But no, she takes a hostage.

"Fox, you and Solly take the other Road Hog. Mary will give you the keys. Harriet and I are headed to the marina now. If you think of anything useful or find Hayley or Fiona, buzz my link immediately."

Solly stepped close to Harriet and pulled her into a hug. "Don't worry," he said softly. "Your

Hayley is a very resourceful little girl. It wouldn't surprise me if she's found a way to escape Fiona's clutches. Have faith."

Harriet returned the hug before stepping away. "Thank you for that." She squeezed her hands into fists until her nails bit into her palms and leaned toward her friend.

"I hope you have plenty of savings, because if Fiona has harmed a single hair on Hayley's head–a single hair–I'm going to kill her. You might need to make my bail."

"Harriet! Let's go."

Alex was already climbing behind the Hog's wheel. Harriet ran to the vehicle while Solly took off after Fox's retreating back. She climbed into the passenger seat and strapped herself in.

Alex drove as fast as he could without endangering the guests, who for some reason seemed to be all over the road that morning. In spite of his frustration at not being able to push the Hog faster, they made good time to the marina. He pulled up in front of the office and leaped from the cab with Harriet close on his heels.

"Leonard!" Fortunately there were no guests inside to hear him yell.

"Do you have anything for me?"

Leonard shook his head as he walked to the counter from where he'd been stocking towels on shelves. "Sorry, no. I've contacted all the dock workers. No red-haired woman has been in here since I received your call twenty minutes ago."

"She has Hayley," Harriet told him. She was afraid of what Fiona might do and completely frustrated because she couldn't take action. Where was the bitch?

"Ah, no. That sweet little girl? Now why would she go and do a thing like that?"

Before Harriet could answer, the speaker on the marina's comm unit crackled and a man's voice spoke.

"Leonard? Yo, man. Got your message. I gave that redhead woman one of the speed boats like you requested, but are you sure about that? She sure didn't act like she knew what she was doing when she drove off."

Leonard grabbed the mic. "Aron? What red-headed woman? I haven't requested a boat for anyone this morning."

Harriet heard some swearing. "Sorry, boss. I thought it was a little strange not hearing from you, but I had the comm–ah, shit. I've had the comm off and on all morning cause I was cleaning below deck and I like to listen to music, you know?"

"Aron . . ."

"She said it was a spur of the moment thing

and you were busy with a bunch of guests so I didn't question it too close, you know? Sometimes that happens. She looked like a guest, else why would she be here? Am I in trouble?"

Harriet heard the tension and worry in Aron's voice.

Leonard ignored Aron. He had raised a screen imbedded in the counter and activated the program used to keep track of the resort's power and sail boats as well as the jet skis.

"Here," he said, jabbing a finger at a dot moving away from the island. "It's too fast to be one of the sailboats and it's the only motorboat showing up that's not moored at the docks. Jet skis have a different signal." He looked upset.

"I'm sorry, Alex. Aron was cleaning inside a cruiser and apparently had his comm off when I called even though it's against the rules. Sorry." He shook his head. "Between this and selling sex without a license I'm going to have to let that boy go. Too bad, he's great at detail work."

"We need a boat," Alex said.

"On it. Head to the docks. I'll inform Aron."

"Don't be too hasty with Aron," Alex said on his way out the door. "He's young yet, and as you say, a good worker."

Harriet followed Alex out of the office and toward the docks. "I'm coming with you," she told him.

"Of course you are. Put this on." He grabbed two life vests from the locker at the head of the power boat dock and handed one to Harriet, then donned his own.

A fit young man with thick blonde hair already held the untied mooring line of one of the marina's fastest boats when they ran down the dock. He had the engine running and tossed the painter into the boat as soon as Alex and Harriet boarded, then ran to the bow line and untied it.

"She has about a twenty minute head start," he told Alex as he tossed the second line into the boat. "But this baby can catch her easy, especially since I don't think the lady knows what she's doing."

Alex waved his thanks and carefully guided the power boat away from the docks. It was fortunate that he was familiar with the boat, having used it once before to rescue Harriet and a companion after they'd been left to drown on Halfway Rock.

"Sit tight." He waited for Harriet to settle into the co-pilot's chair before he gunned the motor. The hydrogen powered engine made no sound, but the boat's bow kicked up into the air as it leapt forward, then settled as they began to fly over the water. Harriet grabbed on to a handle conveniently placed in front of her as she was pressed back into her seat.

They hit waves from the incoming tide once they were well clear of the marina. The bow of the boat rose on the crests and slapped down hard in the troughs but Alex didn't let up on the speed despite the discomfort.

Alex pulled his link from his pocket and handed it to her.

"Call Leonard. Ask him which direction, then stay on the line with him so he can guide us until we get a visual."

Harriet did as instructed, grateful for something to do. She relayed directions from Leonard to Alex, grabbed the binoculars from their nook in the dash, and began to search for the other boat.

"Oh no."

"What? What do you see?"

Harriet lowered the binoculars.

"Aron didn't say anything about a little girl. Fiona must not have had Hayley with her. He would have mentioned if she had a little girl with her. Wouldn't he?" Fear and despair made her voice rise to a thin squeak.

"Not necessarily, Harriet. You might have caught on that Aron isn't very observant. Or

Fiona could have hidden Hayley aboard the boat before she approached Aron."

He nodded at his link. "Ask Leonard to contact Aron and confirm."

Harriet's voice shook when she asked the question. It was a long minute before Leonard came back to tell them that Fiona had been alone when she boarded the boat.

"She could have hid Hayley aboard first, then sought out Aron," Alex repeated.

Harriet shook her head. "No. I can't see that. Fiona has what she came here for. She'll want to get away from the island and your murder investigation as quickly as possible. Fox was right–dragging Hayley along would only slow her down. She either left Hayley behind intentionally or Hayley escaped her."

Was it possible for a little slip of a girl to escape a grown woman? Her throat tightened and she had to blink back tears as she scanned the horizon for Fiona's boat. Fiona had disposed of Hayley. Else why intentionally leave behind her hostage? When they got back to the island they'd be searching for a body.

"Harriet." Alex pulled her from her brooding. "Give me the link. Keep scanning for the boat." He called Fox and told him to start a new hunt for

Hayley once he was sure she wasn't at the air pad. He handed the link back to Harriet.

"We'll find her," he said firmly. "And we'll find her alive and well. Contact Leonard again, make sure we're still on the right course."

"Leonard said to tell you that Fiona is heading straight for Halfway Rock. He said we're at half tide and you'd better hurry." Harriet frowned. "What does he mean?"

Alex checked the chart he'd brought up on the cockpit video display and adjusted their course slightly. "You remember Halfway Rock. What happens to it?"

Harriet had vivid memories of Halfway Rock. She and a friend had been left there to drown not long after she first arrived on the island.

"Oh! The rock will be covered with water. If Fiona tries to drive over it now–"

"She'll rip the bottom out of the boat," Alex finished for her. "Do you see her yet?"

Harriet lifted the binocs back to her face and scanned. "Yes!" She pointed ahead of them. "There she is! She–she's not moving."

Leonard's voice squawked through the link she'd set on the dash.

"She's grounded, Alex. You'd better get to her before she sinks. I'm sending a chopper to lift the boat and bring it back to the marina since you won't be able to tow it."

It took them another five minutes to reach Halfway Rock. Fiona sat on the tip of the boat's bow. The heavier aft end was already under water. She waved with both arms when she spied their boat, then stopped when they drew close enough for her to recognize them.

Alex idled the engine and slowly circled the wreckage.

Harriet could hear the trashed boat's bottom scraping across the rock. Small wavelets slapped against the hulls of both boats. The sun glared off the water and turned the sky a pale, milky blue. An onshore breeze had also risen, gently lifting pieces of her hair that had worked loose from her braid away from her face.

She saw the terror on Fiona's face and felt not even the tiniest bit of sympathy. The script writer clutched a bulging backpack to her chest.

"Can you swim?" Alex called out.

"No! No. You have to save me."

"Where's Hayley?" Harriet shouted. "What have you done with Hayley? Is she on the boat with you?" She saw a sly look cross Fiona's face and knew the woman was about to tell a disgusting lie.

"She's down below. I tied her up and put her

in the cabin below. She'll drown if you don't hurry."

A larger wave pushed against the wrecked boat and it settled deeper in the water. Fiona shrieked and tried to inch higher on the steeply slanted bow.

"The tide's coming in," Alex said mildly. "Pretty soon your boat will sink entirely. Are you sure you want to play games with us? I'd just as soon leave you here to drown, problem solved. Or you could answer a few questions and I'll consider taking you back to the island alive."

Fiona's arms tightened on the backpack.

"Alex," Harriet whispered. "Do you think Hayley is on that boat?"

Alex leaned over to speak into her ear. "No. I think you were right. Hayley escaped Fiona on the island."

"Okay. Okay then." Harriet nodded. "Good. Let's hurry up here so we can get back and join the search."

"Patience. We need information and we'll never be in a better position to get it."

"Miss Sprite." Alex maneuvered their craft so the tide wouldn't push them into the wrecked boat and held it there with small adjustments. If Harriet hadn't been so worried about Hayley she might have appreciated the finesse with which he handled the speedboat.

"Miss Sprite, how did you know Frank Davis and Holden?"

Fiona hesitated. The bow rocked slightly beneath her and settled a few inches deeper in the water.

"We were at the same orphanage together in Ohio. Now get me off this boat."

"Did you kill them?"

"No."

As if it was intentionally aiding Alex's interrogation, the boat jerked beneath Fiona and she slid down the slanted deck toward the water.

"Help me!" she shouted. She grabbed at the bow rail and tried to scramble back up the bow.

"Did you kill Frank Davis and the fire eater named Holden?" Although Alex was happy to let Fiona believe he'd let her drown, he had every intention of rescuing her. He wanted answers first, though, and was willing to let her end up in the water before he threw her a life ring.

"No. Holden killed Frank. I don't know who killed Holden. I swear."

"You were at the circus the night Holden died," Harriet pointed out. "We saw you coming from the Big Tent right before Holden died."

The boat shifted lower and water began to lap at Fiona's sandals.

Fiona glared at them both. "All right. Yes. Yes, I killed them both. Satisfied? Now get me off this stinking boat."

"Where is Hayley?" Harriet asked. "What did you do with her?"

"The brat got away from me. I don't know where she is. I didn't have time to chase after her."

Relief swept through Harriet. She believed Fiona, which meant that Hayley was somewhere on the island. Maybe not safe, maybe hurt, but definitely better off than drowning inside the wrecked boat.

The whump-whump of chopper blades sounded in the distance.

Alex had the confession he needed. It was time to rescue Fiona. He circled Halfway Rock to the windward side and tossed a life ring toward the scuttled boat. It floated toward Fiona until it bumped gently against her hull.

Fiona looked at the white ring in disbelief. "I'm not getting on that thing. Come get me."

Alex shook his head. "No. Too risky. Grab onto the ring and we'll pull you aboard. That's the best we can do."

He had his hands full holding the boat against

the wind and racing tide. Everything was sapping too much energy. The lack of food and sleep was becoming more and more noticeable.

"Hurry up or we're leaving!"

Fiona heard the chopper coming and looked up. "I'll just catch a ride with them."

"That won't be possible. They're going to use large hooks to grab onto the hull. There's no way you'll be able to ride it back to the island."

CHAPTER TWENTY-FOUR

The whump-whump of the chopper continued to grow louder. Harriet could clearly see it now, a black smudge skimming above the crests of the waves.

The waves seemed to realize they had the scuttled boat at their mercy and they pushed harder at its carcass. Keeping their boat off the wreck took all of Alex's concentration. He needed to get Fiona off the wreckage before the chopper reached them.

"Come on, Fiona," he called. "If you wait much longer you're going to be in the water anyway."

Fiona's face paled with fear. She chewed on her lower lip as she looked between the approaching chopper and the white life ring.

"Dammit." Sliding her hand along the bow rail, she slowly worked her way down to the water. A wave hit the partially submerged deck and splashed into her face. She spluttered and tried to climb back up the bow but her sandals couldn't grip the wet surface.

"Leave your pack," ordered Alex.

Fiona's arm tightened on the pack. "Never. It's mine."

She released the bow rail and slid both arms through the back pack straps so the pack sat on her chest. Grabbing the life ring with both hands, she gingerly lay across it. She tried to scream and took in a mouthful of water when her weight pushed the ring below the water's surface.

"Hold on to the ring! We'll pull you in."

Alex nudged the boat a little closer. "Harriet, I need to stay at the helm. Can you manage?"

Harriet had sized up the situation and was already hauling on the life ring's line.

"I have it."

Fiona did nothing to help the process. When the ring bumped against their boat she tried to stand on it to reach the deck, but she overbalanced and fell in. Harriet thought she was going to have to jump in after her but Fiona managed to grab the ring with one hand as she fell. She pulled herself to the surface, choking and gasping for air.

"Help me!" she demanded.

"Give me the backpack before it pulls you under." Harriet reached down to take the pack. Fiona grabbed her hand instead.

"Pull me up. Pull me up."

Fiona Sprite was not a small woman. The combination of her body weight and whatever was in the backpack was too much for Harriet. She could feel the strain on her shoulder and wrist joints.

"*Let go* and give me your back pack. You're too heavy for me to pull in."

"Then get your boyfriend to pull me in."

Harriet shook her head. "I can't do that. Alex is handling the boat. And I'm not strong enough to haul you in with that pack. Looks like we have a stalemate."

Red hair plastered to her skull, Fiona glared up at Harriet with hatred. Grasping the life ring tightly with one arm, she slid her other arm free, then switched arms, but she couldn't lift the pack high enough for Harriet to grab.

"Oh, for crying out loud." Harriet slipped one leg over the gunwale and squeezed tight with her thighs. She leaned down until she could reach the pack. The thing was far heavier than she expected and she almost dropped it.

"What on earth is in here?" She flung it onto

the deck behind her. "Alex! I don't think I'm strong enough to pull Fiona into the boat."

"Check the compartment under the seat on the port side. There might be a ladder in there." Alex pointed to the thin outline of a door under one of the bench seats that Harriet hadn't noticed.

The short aluminum ladder from the compartment fit over the gunwale and hung just above the water's surface. Fiona grabbed for it and hauled herself into the boat.

"You're welcome," Harriet said, putting more than a little disgust in her voice when Fiona displayed zero gratitude for her rescue. Even her young orphans displayed more manners than Fiona.

She put the ladder away and hauled in the life ring. Focused on the task, she wasn't prepared when the boat shot forward. The sudden movement flung her into the stern. She banged her hip on the motor and barely managed to grab onto the transom to keep from going overboard into the water.

"What–" She turned around in time to catch Fiona trying to push an unconscious Alex over the side. The heavy back pack sat near Fiona's feet. If Fiona had bashed Alex with the pack, the thing was heavy enough to have crushed his skull.

A white-hot rage flushed through Harriet. She grabbed up the life ring and rushed at Fiona. Before Fiona could defend herself, Harriet shoved the ring down over Fiona's head and shoulders and onto her arms.

"No!" Fiona squirmed and tried to grab at Harriet but the life ring pinned her arms to her sides.

Harriet grabbed Fiona's upper arms and pushed her toward the stern of the boat. Fiona stumbled and fell and rolled between the seats. The life ring rope wound around her body and legs, trussing her as effectively as a cocoon.

"Alex?"

The wind had picked up and the waves were much larger than they'd been on their way to Halfway Rock. With no one at the helm the boat had turned broadside to the waves. It was getting rocked side to side ever more violently. A wave splashed over the port gunwale and sloshed across the deck.

A second wave rocked the boat. Alex slid further over the gunwale. One more wave and he'd be in the water.

Harriet grabbed Alex's arm and struggled to pull him back into the pilot's seat. He slumped to the side and started to slide out again.

"Oh lord, oh god, help me." The seriousness

of their situation mde her breath catch.

Alex needed medical attention.

More immediate, if she didn't get control of the boat they would swamp and sink. They would all drown if she didn't do something fast.

Bracing her body against the boat's rocking, Harriet pushed Alex back into the seat and pressed her forearm against him to hold him in place.

Another wave hit the side of the boat and splashed in her face. Water sloshed at her feet.

"I'm drowning!" Fiona yelled from behind her.

Truly frightened now, Harriet pivoted to face forward and pressed her backside against Alex to hold him in the seat. She grabbed both the throttle and the helm and said a prayer. She had never driven a boat before, but she knew being broadside to the waves would not end well.

With only a few hiccups, she managed to turn the wheel until she had the boat heading into the waves again and adjusted their speed until they were moving just fast enough to hold their position.

"Alex. Alex, wake up." She didn't dare take her hands off the helm. Behind her, Alex groaned.

"Wake up. I don't know what I'm doing. I need help. Alex!"

"Jeezus, my head feels like I was beaned with a

brick."

Relief coursed through Harriet. "More like a back pack filled with treasure. Are you okay to take over here?"

"Give me a minute." Alex gingerly felt his skull and discovered a large knot behind his left ear. Fiona never should have been able to attack him. Obviously he was off his game from lack of sleep. If he'd been sharp he would have put her in restraints as soon as she boarded the boat. He'd been focused on guiding the boat instead of focused on his prisoner. That was the kind of mistake a rookie would make.

Even worse, he'd put Harriet in danger.

"Where are we?"

Harriet glanced briefly back at him. "We're quite a way from Halfway Rock. Unfortunately we're headed out to sea, although we're moving as slowly as I dare. I'm afraid to turn the boat around. We almost got swamped earlier."

Alex tried to focus his thoughts. His head felt as if someone was tapping it none too gently with a sledgehammer. He was pretty sure he had a concussion.

"Where's Fiona?"

With her eyes focused on the waves splashing against the bow of the boat, Harriet jerked her head. "Back there. Firmly trussed."

Alex started to turn his head, but changed his mind when the pain made spots dance in front of his eyes and his stomach roil.

"Good job. I'm not going to be able to take over the helm."

Panic filled Harriet.

"Alex, I've never handled a boat before. Everything I know I learned from reading fiction books. Fiction! You *have* to take over. I can't do this."

Alex heard the panic in Harriet's voice. He realized that she was pressing back against him to hold him in the helm seat. Embarrassed, he forced himself to sit up straight. He fully intended to tell her he was fine, but a wave of dizziness crashed through him.

He wrapped his arms around her waist to hold himself upright and waited for the dizziness to pass.

"Alex?"

The boat dipped into a trough between waves. He swallowed hard against the sour bile rising in his throat.

"Alex? I can't do this." Harriet's hands shook on the controls. She gripped the wheel tighter.

The bile receded and Alex took a relieved breath. "We'll be fine. I'm going to guide you. We'll do this together." They both ignored Fiona, who was squawking at them from the stern.

Harriet took in a deep breath and let it out. Alex was with her. She could do this with Alex's guidance.

"Okay. What do I do first?"

"Find the knob labeled 'Bilge Pump' and pull it."

Once they had the boat turned toward shore, Alex had Harriet increase their speed until the waves no longer threatened to roll over the transom. They were almost back to the marina when the chopper passed them flying low, the wrecked boat hanging by two foot-wide straps wrapped around its hull.

Harriet knew someone must have lowered themselves into the water from the chopper to set up the straps. Apparently Fiona realized it as well. She yelled and swore at Harriet and Alex for the remainder of the journey back to the docks.

Much to Harriet's relief, the waves smoothed out in the protected marina.

"Okay, you're in position. Cut the engine and glide into the dock," Alex instructed. Harriet shut down the engine and held her breath as the boat bumped a little too hard against its padded berth.

Aron stood on the finger dock waiting for them. He quickly secured the boat and helped Harriet onto the dock. Alex refused a hand, then wished he hadn't acted so proud. Standing made him dizzy and trying to walk made his head pound with every beat of his heart.

"What about *her*?" Aron jerked his head toward Fiona lying in the stern, still trussed in the life ring's line. He pointed a finger at her.

"You got me in a lot of trouble with my boss, you know," he said. "I could lose my job 'cause of you."

Fiona rolled her eyes and scowled. "Big deal. Alert the media. I stole a boat. You don't know what trouble is. Try murdering a person or two and we'll have something to talk about."

Aron's jaw dropped open. "You *stole* the boat? That's–that's–that's not cool, man. That is *not* cool."

Fiona rolled her eyes. "Moron."

"Harriet, where's my link?" Alex leaned against a piling, fighting to stay upright and to resist the urge to escape the pain in his skull with sleep. He needed to take care of business first. He needed to get hold of Fox.

"Ah, your link must still be in the boat. I lost track of it." Harriet climbed back in, found the link jammed beneath the pilot's seat, and set it and the back pack onto the dock.

"Hey, that's *my* pack. Keep your grubby hands off it." Everyone ignored Fiona.

"Call Fox," Alex said. "Tell him to come get

our prisoner and lock her up until I can set up transport to the mainland."

Harriet gave Alex a worried look as she made the call. He looked unnaturally gray beneath his tan. His eyes were glazed and sweat beaded his brow and upper lip. As soon as she rung off with Fox she called Dr. Clarke and asked her to come to the docks to check out a probable concussion.

"Why don't you see what two lives and a stolen boat bought while we wait for Fox to get here?" Alex nodded toward the back pack and immediately wished he hadn't as a fresh wave of pain rolled through his skull. He slid down until he was seated on the rough, weathered planks of the dock and leaned against the piling. Embarrassing to show weakness, but less embarrassing than keeling over into the water would be.

Harriet gave him another worried look, then squatted next to the back pack and undid the fastenings.

"Leave that alone! It's mine! You have no right." Fiona struggled to sit up but was too tangled in the life ring and line to move. She kicked her feet against the stern in frustration.

"That's mine! *I'm* the one who figured out the map was authentic. *I* did all the work. The treasure rightfully belongs to me."

Ignoring Fiona, Harriet reached into the pack

and pulled out a blackened metal box with partially rusted hinges. A hand-forged hasp secured the box. It had been wired shut with wire she recognized as much more modern than the box, even though the wire was also spotted with rust.

A stylized "BB" had been scratched onto the lid.

"BB for Black Bart?" suggested Leonard over her shoulder. She hadn't noticed his arrival.

"That's a good guess. Maybe something inside will tell us."

Although not large enough to qualify as a treasure chest, the box felt heavy enough to be filled with a fortune in gold.

Harriet's hands shook as she worked the wire from the hasp. Everyone on the dock fell silent, even Fiona. Harriet pulled the last bit of wire from the hasp, took a deep breath, and lifted the lid.

"I can't believe people died for this," she whispered, and promptly burst into tears.

Leonard squatted down beside her. He pulled six crumbling, gold colored bricks from the box and lined them up neatly on the dock in front of Harriet.

"They're the right color," he noted, "but these bricks are for building houses." He looked down at Fiona. "Looks like someone got to the treasure before you, Miss Sprite."

Harriet caught a bright glint of gold among the crumbled brick pieces in the bottom of the box. "There's something else in the box." She brushed off the loose debris and pulled out an old gold coin.

"Wow. A real piece of treasure." Leonard's eyes widened. "Can I have a look?"

Harriet handed him the coin. "Do you know what it is?"

Leonard turned the coin over and ran his fingers lightly over its surface.

"It looks authentic," he said slowly. "I can't make out a date, but there's some type of cross on one side." He handed the coin back to Harriet. "You'll have to take it to an expert. I'm sure it's valuable. Nice find."

Harriet stood and tucked the coin into her front pocket. "It's not mine, but I'll have it authenticated and appraised for the owner."

Dr. Clarke arrived on the heels of Fox and Solly and the excitement of the coin was forgotten while Fiona and Alex were dealt with.

Fox replaced Harriet's makeshift restraint with official restraints and loaded a sputtering Fiona into the back of his Road Hog.

Dr. Clarke confirmed Harriet's suspicions.

Alex had a nasty concussion. The doctor insisted that Alex accompany her back to the spa where she could keep an eye on him while she attended to her regular duties. Solly and Harriet helped Alex into the doctor's cart.

"I'll come to the spa as soon as we find Hayley," Harriet promised him.

Alex groaned. "Hayley. I forgot all about her. I can't go to the spa, Doctor. Harriet needs my help." He tried to climb back out of the cart but a wave of dizziness stopped him cold.

"I'm sorry, Harriet. I can't–"

"Shhh." Harriet pushed him gently back into the seat. "Solly and I know what to do, and Fox will give us a hand as soon as he has Fiona secured. Right now you need to do what Dr. Clarke tells you. I'll come see you when we find Hayley."

Alex didn't like it, not one little bit, but he felt too weak and dizzy to argue.

"I want to know as soon as she's found," he complained, then immediately cringed inwardly. He sounded like a whiny kid.

Harriet suppressed a smile and kissed his cheek.

"I promise I will contact you the minute we find her. We've got this."

Alex was still frowning and grumbling when the doctor drove away.

CHAPTER TWENTY-FIVE

Harriet turned to Solly as soon as the doctor drove off with Alex.

"Fiona said Hayley got away from her but she wouldn't say where. Did you and Fox search the entire air pad?"

"We did. Every nook and cranny like Alex instructed. Walk and talk."

They set off toward the Road Hog Alex and Harriet had left parked by the marina office. The cries of seagulls mixed with the laughter and shouts of children learning how to use the sailboards.

The sun felt warm on Harriet's head and shoulders. All was normal–and yet it was not. A little girl was missing and had to be terrified.

"My biggest fear is that Hayley escaped on the

road and is lost somewhere in the jungle." Harriet jumped into the Hog's passenger seat and turned to look at Solly. "If that's the case we might never find her."

Before she realized what he was doing, Solly flicked his finger hard against Harriet's forehead. "That's enough of that talk."

"Ow." Harriet rubbed the spot and glared at her friend. Years before, Solly would flick her when he thought she was acting or talking stupid. She didn't like them any more now than she had then.

"Haven't you been telling me all week how smart those three girls are?"

"Yes, but–"

"*No buts.*" Solly whipped out of the marina. It had been a while since he'd driven anything faster than the resort carts and he felt a little frisson of joy behind the Hog's wheel.

"Let's assume that Hayley escaped and hid from Fiona. Fiona wouldn't have wasted a lot of time looking for her. She would have wanted to get off the island as quickly as possible. Right?" He looked at Harriet and raised his eyebrows in question.

"Yes. Yes, you're right. Fiona pretty much said she didn't waste any time looking for Hayley when she ran off."

Solly couldn't hold back a smug smile. "I do love it when I'm right. So, Hayley wasn't at the air pad, and if she was hiding near the marina she would have gone to the office once she saw Fiona take off in the boat. She knows Leonard and wouldn't be afraid of him."

"Okay. Yeah." Harriet began to race through the possibilities in her mind. "She might have headed back to the amusement park to look for Dorian and Amber Lee."

Solly shook his head. "I don't think so. If she'd done that, someone would have spotted her by now. There were a lot of people looking for the three girls. Even the guests were keeping their eyes open."

Frustrated, Harriet drummed her fingers on her thighs and stared blindly at the jungle edging the road. She was tired and hungry and her wrist and shoulder ached from Fiona yanking on her arm.

Poor Hayley must be famished by now. Where was she? Was she cowering somewhere, afraid to show herself? The thought of Hayley cowering under some jungle bush, hungry and alone and crying, made Harriet's stomach knot.

Solly interrupted her thoughts. "Given her smarts, I think that Hayley would stick to the road–maybe hide if she heard a cart coming–but

I'm confident that she wouldn't take off into the jungle. It can be scary for an adult. Imagine how a young child would feel. We can knock that off our list of places to look."

"Maybe she's back at the hotel. I'll call the desk." Harriet pulled a link from her pocket.

"Crap, I forgot to give Alex his link. He'll be lost without it."

Solly looked at the link in her hand. "I doubt that Alex is in any condition to make or receive calls."

Harriet nearly dropped the link when it suddenly buzzed in her hand.

"Hello?"

There was silence on the line.

"Hello?"

"My apologies. I must have the wrong number," said a slightly accented male voice.

"This is Harriet Monroe. I have Alex Hayes's link. Were you trying to reach Alex?"

"Yes. We have a small situation here."

"Alex is out of touch at the moment. Who is this? Perhaps I can contact someone who can help."

"Could you send someone to the circus please?"

Harriet looked at the silent link in her hand. "He disconnected but I recognized the voice. That was Sugo from the circus. He wants Alex to come to the circus."

"Fox is tied up at the moment. We might as well swing by on our way to the hotel and see if we can help. We're almost there now," Solly pointed out when Harriet tried to protest. "And there's no one else."

"Fine." There really wasn't any point in arguing since Solly was already pulling into the circus parking space. Harriet debated leaving Solly to deal with Sugo's problem while she took the Hog to the hotel, but Solly anticipated her and pulled the keys from the ignition.

"We'll *both* go see what Sugo wants."

Harriet grumbled a few choice insults but Solly merely shook his head and guided her to the gate where Tamara waved them through. Harriet would have preferred to ask Tamara what the problem was, but she was busy answering questions from a family with seven boisterous children.

Salina the stilt walker waved to Harriet but didn't approach them.

They passed the Big Tent and the game and food cabanas to the rear of the circus grounds where they found Sugo pacing back and forth outside the lion's home tent. He rushed toward them and grabbed Harriet by her sore arm. She bit her lip to keep from crying out at the unexpected pain.

"Come with me." He pulled Harriet into the tent without waiting for an answer.

Resort guests and employees were not allowed inside the animals' home tents, and other than the visit to the dog tent the previous night with Alex, Harriet had adhered to that restriction even though she suspected that she would be welcomed anywhere.

It took her eyes several long minutes to adjust from the bright sunshine to the dimmer tent interior. Despite being in a hurry to look for Hayley, she was curious about where the lions lived. The first thing that struck her was the smell. She noticed the strong, musky scent of the big cats mixed with the faint smell of raw meat.

"I found her a half hour ago."

"What?" Harriet squeezed her eyes shut for the count of three. When she opened them she saw the lion cage filling most of the center of the tent. Both lions were lying on their sides sleeping, if the deep, rhythmic snoring was any indication.

Nestled against the side of one of the big cats was a small, dark-skinned child.

"Hayley!"

"Shhhh," urged Sugo. "I have fed Regis and Apollo a mild tranquilizer but they are not unconscious. They are old and tranqs can be very dangerous for them. I tried to talk the young lady out of the cage but she insists the lions will protect her from a 'bad lady'." He turned a questioning look on Harriet.

"How on earth did she get inside the cage?" Harriet asked. "Never mind, it's not important. We have to get her out of there."

"I agree. My boys are old and docile but they might feel that they have to protect their home. They will wake up soon."

Harriet stepped up next to the cage, knelt down so she was on the same level as Hayley, and grabbed the bars.

"Hayley," she called softly. She could see that Hayley's eyes were scrunched too tight for her to be asleep. She was most likely faking it for Sugo's benefit. Fine, she would play along.

"Hay-ley, wake up. It's time to go home. Dorian and Amber Lee are waiting for you. Come on, sweetheart. Time to go."

Hayley opened her eyes. She squealed when she saw Harriet. "Mizz Mun-row! You'll never guess what happened!"

Regis–or was it Apollo?–snorted and twitched a giant paw.

"Shhh. The lions are sleeping, Hayley. You don't want to wake them, do you?"

Hayley crawled on her hands and knees to where Harriet knelt.

"They protected me from that bad lady," she said in a loud whisper. Hayley's accusing eyes locked on Harriet's face. "You said she was a friend."

Harriet shook her head. Guilt mixed with fear for Hayley's safety. She didn't know how long Hayley had been hiding in the lion's cage, but it was a miracle they hadn't mauled the child.

"I was wrong. Miss Sprite is definitely not our friend. I apologize. You need to come out of there *now,* so I can show you how sorry I am."

"Okay." Hayley stuck a leg and shoulder between two bars of the cage.

"Oh, wait." She pulled back inside the cage and returned to the sleeping lion and gave him a hug and a pat on the cheek. One amber colored eye opened.

"Hayley, come out of there right now."

The lion lifted his head off the cage floor and regarded Harriet. She could swear he was telling her not to sweat it, especially when he yawned widely, revealing the longest teeth she'd ever seen, and lay back down.

Hayley popped through the bars and threw herself into Harriet's arms, knocking her back.

"You know what?"

"What?"

"The bad lady took our treasure. She made Dorian and Amber stay in the cave."

"I have good news for you, poppet. We found Amber Lee and Dorian and they're waiting for you at the hotel." Harriet stood and hefted Hayley onto her hip. Looking much relieved, Sugo held the tent flap open for her.

"I suggest you redesign that cage and place the bars a little closer together," she told him on her way out.

Sugo bowed his head slightly. "I'll see to it."

She could see that Solly had been pacing outside the tent. "Sugo wouldn't let me in," he explained, hurrying over to them. "He was afraid too many strangers in their home would upset the lions."

"Hayley, have you met my friend Solomon Ayers?"

Hayley pursed her lips and regarded Solly. She shook her head.

"No, is he a *real* friend?"

"He is my *best* friend–just like Dorian and Amber Lee are your best friends," Harriet assured the girl.

Solly smiled. "Hello, Hayley. It's very nice to meet you. Harry has told me a lot about you."

Hayley lowered her chin and fluttered her lashes at Solly.

Harriet didn't know whether to laugh or groan. Solly's good looks had always inspired females of all ages to flirt with him.

She gave Hayley the once-over, looking for injuries. Hayley's tee shirt had a tear. Her clothes and bare feet were filthy and she had a long scratch on one calf–all of which could be cleaned up at the hotel. Hayley chattered non-stop all the way to the hotel, apparently nowhere near as traumatized as Harriet had imagined her to be.

A half hour later Hayley sat in a hot bath with perfumed bubbles. Amber Lee and Dorian hung on the side of the tub keeping a close eye on her. Fox had arrived and sat in the suite's living area with Solly, waiting for Harriet to fill him in on what she knew.

Before she could begin, there was another knock on the door. Harriet opened it and found a worried Payson standing in the hall.

"Are the missing girls all right?" he asked, before Harriet could even greet him.

"Come in. I was just about to fill Tarbell in, and yes, all three girls are doing fine. Hayley is enjoying her moment in the spotlight. Sugo found her in the lion cage, you know."

Payson shook his head. "We'll have to make

some modifications to that cage," he muttered as he walked into the suite and took a chair.

Harriet suppressed a grin. "I said the same thing. I think Hayley took a decade off Sugo's life when he found her snuggled up to one of his fierce beasts."

Once they were all settled, Harriet began at the beginning with the murder of Frank Davis and ended with talking Hayley out of the lion's cage. When she came to the bit about opening the treasure box and finding old bricks, she saw Payson smirk.

"You knew about the treasure, didn't you?" she accused.

Payson smiled, his pale blue eyes twinkling. "Douglas found it decades ago. Of course the chest held a real treasure back then. As I understand it, some of Black Bart's crew mutinied when they were attacked by another pirate. They set fire to Bart's ship after unloading most of the gold and sailed off in the second ship, leaving Bart and a handful of his crew to perish.

"Bart escaped the burning ship in a dinghy with a small chest of gold that the other pirate had missed and buried it in the cave. He was rescued after spending a year on the island. No sign of the other crew members."

"That's a great story," Solly said. "I bet Black

Bart killed off the rest of his crew so they couldn't reveal where he buried the gold. What did Mr. Wade do with the treasure?"

"He used it to start his business empire and buy this island."

Harriet remembered the gold coin in her pocket. She pulled it out and handed it to Payson.

"Maybe you could see that Mr. Wade gets this. He must have missed this coin when he emptied the chest."

Payson held up his hand. "Keep it. Douglas doesn't need it. Or better yet, put it in a safe deposit box for Hayley and her friends. Or have it appraised and sell it to a collector and invest the money in your orphan program."

Harriet rubbed her thumb over the cross on the coin. "I think–it really doesn't belong to me. Do you think that you could sell it and invest the money? Maybe put it into an account for the girls' future use?"

Payson beamed at her. "It would be my pleasure. I'll make us both trustees and stipulate that it be divided evenly three ways when the girls turn twenty-one. Will that suit?"

"It sounds perfect." Harriet handed Payson the coin and this time he took it.

Solly had been listening from the kitchenette where he'd put together a pitcher of lemonade.

He poured four glasses and carried them into the living area where he handed them around. "There's something I still don't understand," he said.

Harriet accepted the drink with appreciation. The cold, sweet and tangy liquid tasted great. She hadn't realized how dehydrated she was.

"What don't you understand?" asked Fox, accepting a glass.

"All the orphanages I've heard about keep the boys separated from the girls. When did Fiona get the chance to become good friends with Frank Davis and Holden?"

"I think I can answer that," Harriet said. She drained her glass and set it on the table beside her seat. "I think when they became friends Fiona was not a Fiona. She changed her name after she left the orphanage and started hormone replacement therapy."

"Ah. That does explain a few things," Fox said, "including why Madame Zaza said we were looking for a woman murderer and then changed her mind and said the murderer was a man."

"Well, that about wraps things up." Payson stood. "I'd best be going. I'll stop and check on Alex on my way back to my cottage."

He was almost at the door when Harriet remembered something and followed him. She stepped out into the hall with Payson and closed the door behind them.

"What's wrong, Harry? Should I be worried?"

"No, it's nothing like that. I have a favor to ask of Mr. Wade." Harriet told him about the teacher at the girls' orphanage who tormented Dorian and how the woman delighted in making the orphans miserable.

"What's her name?"

"Mrs. Barlow."

"Leave it to me. I'll see that she's let go and I'll make sure she doesn't get another job working with children."

"Thank you, and please thank Mr. Wade."

Payson planted a kiss on her cheek. "Will do. By the way, you have an appointment with Dr. Bainbridge next Thursday morning. I'll accompany you and we'll have our Thursday lunch on the mainland." He turned and walked off before Harriet could come up with a reason not to keep the appointment with the head doctor.

"Wily old man," she muttered as she walked back into the suite, then put the appointment out of her mind. She had a very short time left with the girls and Alex needed her. Next Thursday was a long way off.

CHAPTER TWENTY-SIX

Unfortunately Thursday arrived much faster than Harriet was prepared for. After a trip in Wade's private shuttle to the mainland, she sat in a richly decorated waiting room expensively furnished with comfortable leather club chairs. The deep green pile carpet was so thick it felt like walking on a foam cushioned floor. Original art, mostly scenes of Italy, graced the pale gold walls and soft jazz played from hidden speakers.

Two attractive receptionists, a male and a female, typed away at a crescent shaped black marble desk. They spoke softly into headsets, their eyes never leaving the screens in front of them.

"How're you doing?" Alex asked Harriet, speaking low so he wouldn't be overheard.

"Fine."

He frowned. She didn't look fine. She looked tense. And she had that little furrow between her brows that told him she was feeling worried.

He had recovered from his concussion and returned to work several days before. Fiona Sprite, formerly known as Greg Hardy, had been charged with two counts of murder in the first degree and a single charge of kidnapping, and was presently locked up on the mainland awaiting a trial.

Alex sincerely hoped that it would be a very long spell before he worked another murder. The resort island had not turned out to be the trouble free job he had expected when he signed on. Looking on the bright side, an occasional murder was better than multiple deaths every day like he'd faced on the force.

He linked his fingers with Harriet's and squeezed lightly. When he had first spoken to Payson about Harriet's memory loss he had been looking for guidance on the best way to help her. He had readily agreed with Payson's plan to get Harriet seen to by a specialist friend of Payson's. But he was having doubts now that they were here. He didn't know this doctor from Adam. What if he was a jerk? All he had were Payson's reassurances.

Harriet experienced debilitating physical pain

whenever she tried to remember anything before her eighth year. What if the doctor looked upon Harriet as an oddity–a freak? Or a guinea pig? What if the doctor forced her to endure the unendurable simply because he was curious?

Alex took a deep breath and let it out. They were here. It was a little late to be asking questions he should have thought to ask before now.

"Busy place," he remarked.

Harriet rolled her eyes at his comment. The three of them were the only people in the waiting room. She wished she'd accepted the receptionist's offer of something to drink, if only to have something to occupy her while she waited.

"It is busy, actually." Payson turned from the painting he had been studying and looked at Harriet. "People come to this clinic from all over the world."

He had exchanged his less formal island wear for a well-fitted navy suit, white shirt with ultra-thin burgundy stripes, and a navy tie with matching burgundy stripes. His white hair was tied back in a neat queue and his short black boots reflected the sunlight streaming through the large window overlooking a canal.

He looks like a high powered corporate executive, Harriet thought with surprise. She was so used to seeing Payson on the island she hadn't really considered him in what she now thought of as the real world. Judging by how natural he looked in the suit, he obviously felt equally at home in both worlds. It was an unexpected reminder of how little she knew about the man she'd grown to think of as a beneficent uncle.

She realized Payson was looking at her with concern and flushed.

"Edgar is one of the top neurologists in the world, Harry. There's no need to be nervous."

"I'm not nervous," Harriet answered, then realized she was drumming the fingers of her free hand against her thigh–a sure sign of nerves. She wished Solly had come with them. He had asked her if she needed him and she'd told him she'd be fine, but she didn't feel fine.

"Sorry. I just don't know what to expect." She grimaced. "And you're right, I'm feeling a little nervous."

"Dr. Bainbridge will see you now," called the male receptionist. He rose from his seat and held open an unmarked, heavy wooden door at the far end of the room.

Alex stood and pulled Harriet to her feet. "You'll be fine. This is just an assessment to see what's going on in that marvelous head of yours. Nothing's going to happen without your say-so."

He planted a soft kiss on her forehead and hoped he spoke the truth.

"You've got this," he whispered against her hair.

Harriet took a deep breath and pasted a shaky smile on her face. "Right. Let's get this over with." She squared her shoulders and marched toward the waiting receptionist.

"I'll be waiting here for you," Payson assured her.

Harriet whirled around and jabbed a finger toward him. "Oh no, you don't. You two started this and I expect both of you to see it through with me. Otherwise I'm going home." She folded her arms across her chest and glared at Payson, who quickly turned a surprised laugh into a cough.

"Well, if you feel that strongly about it . . ."

"I do."

"All right then. We'll do this together."

Payson hid his relief at Harriet's command that he join her and Alex for the consultation and tests. He had grown deeply fond of Harriet since her arrival on the island and had come to look upon her as the daughter he'd never had. He wanted–*needed*–to be involved, for his own sake as much as Harriet's.

The heavy wooden door closed quietly behind them. They stood in a much more sparsely decorated office, one obviously set up for the actual work of looking into brains.

A modern, green quartz desk, three cushioned visitor chairs covered in a subtle green, pale brown, and red plaid, an examination table, and a chair attached to an imaging machine with a wired helmet that looked straight out of a horror flick were the only furnishings. Harriet suppressed a shudder and forced herself to look away.

Payson glanced briefly at the equipment and prayed the tests would give his friend Edgar a clear path to unlocking Harriet's memory.

Locked up in Harriet Monroe's brain were memories that were important to Payson Douglas Wade. Memories he desperately needed to access. He could never rest easy until he had learned the truth about what had happened to his baby sister–and Harriet was the only person living who knew that truth and could give him those answers.

Hopefully she wouldn't pay too high a price to get them.

I'm glad you found this book out of the millions available. If you'd like to know what else I've written or when I release a new book instead of leaving it to chance, you can sign up for my newsletter or send me an email through my website CharleyMarshBooks.com. I love to hear from my readers.

Watch for the next book in the Destination Death Mystery Series Coming April 2021

Shattered in Paradise

ABOUT THE AUTHOR

In her younger days Charley Marsh's curiosity drove her to climb mountains, canoe rivers, and explore caves and wilderness areas from Maine to California. She's been shot at, caught in a desert flash flood, and almost drowned off the Maine coast. Once she tobogganed down a 5,000+ foot mountain.

Life is always an adventure if you have the right attitude.

Charley never set out to be a storyteller, but looking back on the elaborate lies she made up as a troubled teen she can see that she always had the makings. Now, in the words of Lawrence Block, she happily "makes up lies for fun and profit."

Lightning Source UK Ltd.
Milton Keynes UK
UKHW011036110121
376834UK00005B/1020